AN OFFER OF MARRIAGE

"Now, Miss Woodruff," he said, keeping his voice low and promising himself to keep the exchange very brief, "just how may I be of service to you?"

"I wish for you to marry me, Mr. Mallory," she said, looking him in the eye as she spoke. "Will you do so?"

For a moment, Mallory felt as though someone had just struck the backs of his knees and feared they might buckle beneath him. He understood then just why ladies prone to fainting spells carried smelling salts with them.

He cleared his throat tentatively, wishing for the bracing fumes of some sal volatile. "I beg your pardon, Miss Woodruff. Perhaps I did not understand you properly—"

She smiled at him. "You understood me perfectly well, Mr. Mallory. You simply do not wish to answer me."

—from *The Rebel and the Rogue* by Mona Gedney

BOOK YOUR PLACE ON OUR WEBSITE AND MAKE THE READING CONNECTION!

We've created a customized website just for our very special readers, where you can get the inside scoop on everything that's going on with Zebra, Pinnacle and Kensington books.

When you come online, you'll have the exciting opportunity to:

- View covers of upcoming books
- Read sample chapters
- Learn about our future publishing schedule (listed by publication month *and author*)
- Find out when your favorite authors will be visiting a city near you
- Search for and order backlist books from our online catalog
- Check out author bios and background information
- Send e-mail to your favorite authors
- Meet the Kensington staff online
- Join us in weekly chats with authors, readers and other guests
- Get writing guidelines
- AND MUCH MORE!

**Visit our website at
http://www.kensingtonbooks.com**

Waltz with a Rogue

Kathleen Baldwin
Mona Gedney
Lisa Noeli

ZEBRA BOOKS
KENSINGTON PUBLISHING CORP.
www.kensingtonbooks.com

ZEBRA BOOKS are published by

Kensington Publishing Corp.
850 Third Avenue
New York, NY 10022

All Kensington titles, imprints and distributed lines are available at special quantity discounts for bulk purchases for sales
promotion, premiums, fund-raising, educational or institutional
use.

Special book excerpts or customized printings can also be
created to fit specific needs. For details, write or phone the
office of the Kensington Special Sales Manager: Kensington
Publishing Corp., 850 Third Avenue, New York, NY 10022.
Attn. Special Sales Department. Phone: 1-800-221-2647.

Zebra and the Z logo Reg. U.S. Pat. & TM Off.

First Printing: March 2005
10 9 8 7 6 5 4 3 2 1

Printed in the United States of America

CONTENTS

The Highwayman Came Waltzing

Kathleen Baldwin

Author's Note

Special thanks to my critique partners, extra-ordinaire, for their help with this project.

For more information about the romantic, sometimes brutal, truths behind the real highway-men of myth and legend, please visit my website at www.KathleenBaldwin.com.

Chapter 1

The coachman hesitated at the signpost. Coach lamps flickered through the darkness, casting dim yellow rays on a marker he didn't recall. He frowned, but turned the cumbersome black coach down the left fork of the road, as the sign directed. A dense stand of ancient, gnarled beeches and towering silver birch soon swallowed up the narrow road. The sides of the carriage scraped against the trees. The footman, hanging onto the rear guard, swore softly as he dodged broken twigs and whipping branches.

Passage slowed, until they came to a dead halt at a log fallen across the road. The coachman stared glumly at the offending roadblock.

A distant sound captured his attention. The screech of an owl, or the yip of a fox, would not have startled him. This sound gave him the shivers. Exotic. Faint. The forlorn strains of a flute whispered through the trees.

The door to the carriage banged open, prompting the footman to jump down and hurry to assist his master.

"What's all this then? Why are we stopped?" Sir Godfrey clambered down the steps.

Neither of his servants answered.

"Is that music? Out here?"

The moon peeped out from behind swirling dark clouds. The coachman sucked in his breath. "Cor! Bless me! It's a ghost. There! In the trees." He pointed.

"Rubbish!" Sir Godfrey huffed himself up and started toward the front of the coach. "No such thing as ghosts. Where?"

Feathery laughter rippled like soft wind in Sir Godfrey's ear. "Here. There. Everywhere." A sharp point pricked his neck. "Stand and deliver, monsieur."

"Frenchman!" He uttered it like a curse word. The hapless baron couldn't help but glance sideways, hoping to see if his footman still stood. Alas, there would be no help from that quarter. His quaking servant's arms were pinned securely by a tall masked brute. The footman's wigged head was soon shrouded under a black hangman's hood.

Sir Godfrey sucked in his breath. They were dead men.

Mystical notes from the flute floated through the darkness, like the hypnotic dance of an Arabian princess, swirling her veils through the air, weaving them through the black night, binding their hearts with fear.

Above the coach, a lithe catlike creature leapt down from a low-lying branch onto the box behind the frozen coachman. "Do not move, my friend. Zis is a very light trigger." In a trice, this third brigand covered the coachman's head with a black sack and tied his hands with a violet sash.

Sir Godfrey hissed. "Ruddy French blackguards."

"Back to ze coach, Englishman. Surely, your beautiful wife hungers for your company, no? But first, empty your pockets, *s'il vous plaît.*"

Glowering furiously, Sir Godfrey foraged through his pockets and produced a small leather bag. He held it aloft by the drawstrings, before reluctantly dropping it into the bandit's outstretched palm.

Hefting the bag, weighing its contents, the Frenchy jingled the coins and flashed a wide grin under a scraggly, ill-kept beard. "*Tch, tch,* monsieur. A man like you, a man of ze world, must carry more zan zis pittance. In my country you would not even qualify for ze guillotine for such a . . . how do you say? Paltry sum. Hand over ze other purse."

"Other?"

The Frenchman shrugged. "*C'est la vie.* If you prefer to remove all of your clothing, I will take them and search later."

Sir Godfrey's wife whimpered from the coach. "I told you we should hire outriders. For pity's sake, give him what he wants."

"I'll see you hang for this." Godfrey balled his fists at his sides.

With lightning speed, the masked bandit whipped the short foil to the baron's chest and popped off one of his vest buttons. "*Possiblé.* But not, I zink, before I zee your purse." The sword point moved to the next button.

"Stop that. Those are pearl buttons!"

"Ah! So they are." The bandit chuckled and, in one quick motion, sliced the rest of them from their moorings, caught them, and deposited the pearls in the deep pockets of his black coat.

Uttering a string of curse words unfit for his lady-wife's ears, Sir Godfrey dug out a second bag of money.

"*Merci.*"

From atop the coach, the third thief jumped nimbly down and aimed an antiquated flintlock at their quarry. "I'll guard ziz fat one while you get ze jewels."

The tall highwayman who was tying the moaning footman to the rear of the coach nodded and gruffly scolded, *"Fermé la buche!"*

Sir Godfrey's wife cowered inside the coach, bawling like a small child.

"Your pardon, madam." The bandit swooped off a black tricorn with a purple ostrich feather and bowed lavishly. "I must relieve you of zis stunning necklace." The needle sharp foil raised the string of diamonds from the lady's neck without making a scratch.

Still quaking, the lady obediently reached back and unclasped the diamond collar, dropping it into the bandit's gloved palm. Tears trickled down her cheek.

"No. No. Do not cry, my lady. You are even more beautiful without such bright adornments. I ask you, would you see the beauty of ze moon if ze sun hung beside it? No. *N'cet pas?* Without zeze diamonds blocking the view, your lovely eyes will captivate the gentlemen. *Oui,* your husband, he will have to hire a battalion to protect his exquisite wife from all ze lovesick swains, no?"

The lady brought a hand to her breast and blinked quizzically at the masked thief.

"And now, ze ring, also, madam."

She shook her head and leaned away, clutching her hands together. "No. Please, I beg you. It belonged to my mother. It's all I have left of her. You can't take it from me."

"Is zis true?"

The lady nodded.

"How can I refuse ze request of a loving daughter? Keep ze ring. And now, I bid you, *adieu*." The bandit bowed again, donned the tricorn with a flourish, and turned from the coach doorway.

A shot blasted to shreds the lyrical quality of the night. A scream. Another shot. Two screams. Godfrey's wife added her shrieks to the cacophony. The horses skittered and snorted, jangling their harnesses.

Sir Godfrey held a smoking pistol in his hand. The smallest bandit lay on the ground in front of him. Motionless.

From the shadows, a club descended on Sir Godfrey's head. The blow dropped him to his knees, stunned; an instant later he toppled forward.

The Frenchman ran to the fallen comrade, hoisted the black-clad figure up by the arm, and began dragging the body into the woods. "Bertie, help me."

Bertie grunted, jammed the club back into a sheath, foraged beside the fallen baron for the small pistol, stuffed it into a pocket, and ran to shoulder the other side of the limp body.

Moonlight scarcely penetrated the thick canopy of beech trees. Yet, even in the darkness, the highwaymen ran as if they knew the way by heart. Ahead of them, in a clearing, stood a dilapidated wooden cart hitched to a worn old pony.

Blending with the fog, a woman, slender and willowy, draped in flowing silver-gray, waited beside the rig. She might easily be mistaken for a ghost. "Is it Bonnie?"

"Yes. We must hurry."

The phantom nodded and climbed onto the

back of the horse, a wraith, delicate as the curling fog around them, astride the thickly built pony.

Taking up the reins, the highwayman whistled to the horse. Bertie sat on the rear seat, holding the lifeless bandit across her lap. As the cart rolled ponderously down the rutted path, the ghostly rider leaned forward, stroked the horse's neck, hugged the old pony, and whispered in its pricked ear. The mare snorted, lifted her tired feet higher, and soon the cart was bouncing rapidly toward the Dower House.

Chapter 2

Two days later

Elizabeth sat curled up in the window seat of the upstairs parlor, going over the figures in the accounting book, basking in the relative peace of the afternoon. Her Aunt Bertie sat nearby in her favorite chair, reading the newspaper and humming softly, and her grandmother stitched quietly.

Bonnie charged into the room, swinging her protective vest in one hand and wielding a small hammer in the other. "If I leave the lead ball lodged in the wood, it will make the vest just that much stronger." She stopped directly in front of Elizabeth. It was a question, of course, but Bonnie preferred to make statements open to challenge, rather than beg an answer.

Elizabeth glanced up from her accounting. "If the wood is compromised, you ought to replace the slat as well."

"Oh bother." Bonnie stamped her foot and turned away to plop down on a small stool beside the hearth.

"Altogether too much work. I'll just patch it. Besides, what are the chances of getting shot in the same place twice?"

"Don't say such things!" Elizabeth's aunt Lavinnia stood in the doorway, her hand over her heart. "I should hope you will *never* get shot again. Anywhere."

"No, mother." Bonnie began nailing down a new piece of tin over her punctured one.

"Good. Now, do exactly as Lizzy says. That contraption saved your life." Lavinnia positioned herself on the settee and pulled out a pile of sewing.

Bonnie muttered softly and continued doing a patch job instead of a replacement.

Elizabeth shook her head. Her cousin, Bonnie, had a stubborn streak inherited from their grandmother.

Bonnie's twin sister, Blythe, floated in behind her mother and sat down at the pianoforte. She toyed with nine notes, playing them over and over, rearranging and regrouping them into various melodies, while her twin's hammer tapped incongruously to the harmony.

Aunt Bertie rustled her newspaper and hummed all the louder.

Elizabeth marveled that they could all concentrate irrespective of one another. Apart from the discordant racket in the parlor, she heard a noise outside in the yard and lifted the edge of the lace curtain. Lord Mulvern's coach rolled to a stop. She took a deep breath, set her book down on the table, and hurried across the worn Aubusson rug to her grandmother's chair.

Nana Rose's old straight-backed chair creaked when Elizabeth squatted down and grabbed hold of the arm. "Nana, Lord Mulvern is here. Promise you will be on your best behavior."

Her grandmother stiffened her spine and looked down her nose at Elizabeth. "What can you be saying, Lizzy? I am *always* on my best behavior."

"You know precisely what I mean. Try not to goad him."

"I will speak as I please to the man who murdered my sons and took away my—"

It was an old refrain. One they all knew by heart. "Not today, Nana. Please."

"Why should today be any different? He's still a murderer." Nana Rose nearly spit the words, belying her dignified appearance—starched black bombazine and cloud-white hair coiled up high enough to suit even Marie Antoinette. "Just as Cain slew Able and was punished, so—"

"Yes, of course. But consider the effect one slip of the tongue might have on your granddaughters. We cannot risk it." She patted her grandmother's hand and stood up to survey the rest of their family.

Blythe stopped playing the pianoforte, her face paler than usual.

"No, my dear." Elizabeth shook her head. "You mustn't worry. All will be well. Why don't you keep playing. It relaxes you."

"Yes, widgeon. Don't fret." Bonnie hopped up from her stool, tucked her chest protector into the bottom of the cupboard, and kissed her twin sister on the head. "It'll be a jolly bit of fun to see what he knows."

Blythe did not turn back to the piano keys. Instead, she lowered her eyes and folded her hands in her lap. Her flaxen hair fell forward, a silken curtain behind which she would hide.

Bertie dropped her newspaper to the floor and went to check on the arrival for herself. She stood boldly before the window, as a man might, without the slightest concern for propriety. She drew back the curtains with one hand, while rapping the knuckles of her other impatiently against the wall. "Blast, and double blast. What in blazes is Mulvern doing here?"

Nana Rose sniffed. "Probably got wind of something, the old goat." She didn't look up from the pile of black silk she was stitching. It was hard to distinguish which was the new fabric being sewn and which was that of her flowing black mourning dress.

"Lizzy is right. We must all mind our manners." Lavinnia glanced about the room genially, her frilly white mobcap bobbing cheerfully over her yellow curls. "Bound to visit, isn't he? He's family, after all. A gentlemanly thing to do." She surveyed her twin daughters. "Best foot forward, girls. Do try to smile, Blythe dear."

"Well, I don't like it." Bertie plunked back down into her chair, which hailed from King Henry's reign, and rubbed at the carved claw on the end of the arm. The wood had long ago lost its varnish. "Not a bit of it."

Elizabeth stood in the middle of the room. "We must all stay calm." She adjusted her serviceable brown muslin, hoping to hide the patchwork in the folds of the skirt, and pinched her cheeks. She considered her high cheekbones her only admirable asset. Pinching them was her last remaining bow to vanity.

Footsteps clattered in the entryway, and Lord Mulvern's booming voice echoed up the stairs as he groused at the housemaid. "No need to announce me, girl. Confound it. It's my house after all."

They all listened as their maid stoically insisted

on protocol. "That's as may be, m'lord. But the ladies might require a moment to prepare for visitors." The spry housemaid scampered up the stairs ahead of him and dashed into the parlor. "It's his lordship, mum. And he's brought Master Trace with him."

"Trace? Here?" Elizabeth dropped down on the settee, astonished.

The gentlemen were not long behind. Lord Mulvern's massive height took up most of the doorway. "You see what I must put up with." Removing his hat, exposing a headful of frizzled graying hair, he addressed, not them, but his companion. "Confounded Dower House. Packed to the gills with females. Can't take a step without tripping over a confounded petticoat."

Nana Rose elevated her nose higher into the air. "Pray, do forgive us, your lordship. We will endeavor to go without undergarments if you insist. Indeed, on our current allowance, I'm surprised there's more than one petticoat to be found in the entire house."

Lord Mulvern frowned at his sister-in-law.

Elizabeth stood up and beckoned to him. "Come in, Lord Mulvern. Please be seated." She strained to see past his shoulders to catch a glimpse of Trace. "The maid said your stepson is with you?"

"So he is." Lord Mulvern thumped into the room and took possession of Elizabeth's seat on the settee next to Lavinnia. "With Napoleon tucked away for good this time, Trace's work is done. Sold off his commission. He's come home to hunt down the band of thieves terrorizing our neighborhood."

Elizabeth forgot to breathe as Trace entered the

room. The friend she remembered had changed. There was nothing of the boy left in him. His face no longer held the smooth fullness of youth. Well-defined angles had taken its place. The small parlor filled with the clean scent of his shaving soap and the crisp smell of freshly pressed linen. His bearing was that of an officer in command: robust, regal. She stepped back. Indeed, the self-assurance in his blue eyes made her feel nervous and fascinated all at the same time.

"Trace." Her voice scratched out, scarcely rising above a whisper.

"Lizzy?" He removed his hat, surveying her curiously. "I hope we find you well?"

She nodded, surprised to see his honey brown hair still curling intriguingly around his ears and neck. That, at least, had not changed.

Suddenly, Elizabeth wished she had not drawn her hair back so severely that morning. The single black knot at her neck could not possibly flatter her. She looked down at the ugly brown muslin gown. Oh, why hadn't she worn her other dress? She must look a ghastly old crow.

But what did it matter? What were such foolish thoughts to anything? She was an ape leader, at five and twenty, on the shelf for so many years she had grown moldy. Lord Mulvern's stepson would have no interest in an aging spinster. She smiled with all the dignity she could muster and offered him her hand.

Trace grasped it warmly. "A pleasure to see you again." He said it as if the sentiment almost surprised him.

She swallowed. "Yes. Welcome home." She nervously pulled her hand from his. There were no remaining seats, except the wobbly old spindle-legged chair against the wall. She glanced dubiously at it.

He followed her gaze and without hesitation moved the frail chair forward. "This will serve."

Elizabeth squeezed onto the end of the settee, forcing her Aunt Lavinnia to scoot closer to Lord Mulvern, and folded her hands in her lap. "We've read and reread all the accounts in the papers of your . . ." She faltered, searching for the right words.

Bertie nodded. "Heroism. Well done, lad."

"Yes." Nana Rose cleared her throat, sitting as if her back was tied to a board. "Of course, we might've known of your stepson's accomplishments much sooner were our papers not a month old and missing pages." She glared at Lord Mulvern.

"Twaddle." Lord Mulvern snapped his fingers. "No sense wasting money on a second subscription. Tut tut . . . it's enough I have 'em bundled up and sent over. A simple economy." He adjusted his brocade vest. "As usual, Rose, you've veered from the point. Trace has come home to hunt down our band of French cutthroats."

Lavinnia tilted her head sideways, a hand on her pink cheek. "Oh, but Adrian, they haven't cut any throats! Have they?"

Lord Mulvern leaned over and patted her hand. "No, my dear. A figure of speech. But, I daresay, the blackguards nearly killed Sir Godfrey two nights past."

Bertie turned sharply, suddenly very attentive. "What do you mean, *nearly killed him?*"

"Oh dear." Lavinnia held both hands to her face now. "Will the poor man recover?"

"Yes. Yes. Not to worry. He's fine. Nothing to it,

save a lump the size of Mount Vesuvius on the back of his head. The good news is ole Godfrey shot one of the brigands—dead."

"Dead?" Bonnie nearly tipped over on her three-legged stool as she leaned forward, her eyes wide with interest. "Did you find a body? Were there great pools of blood in the road?"

"Bonnie." Elizabeth called her reckless cousin to task.

Lord Mulvern harrumphed. "Quite right. Oughtn't discuss such gruesome things in mixed company."

Elizabeth shot Bonnie a warning glance.

Lord Mulvern continued with his subject. "Point is, can't have these confounded thieves terrorizing m'neighborhood. Trace'll get to the bottom of it."

"Hardly *terrorizing* the neighborhood." Bertie interjected.

"Doing a jolly good job of frightening my guests. Hanging sacks over their heads. Guns. Swords. Enough to scare the life out of 'em, I can tell you that." Mulvern frowned at Bertie.

"What were the sacks made of, do you know?" Nana Rose actually sounded pleasant for once.

Lord Mulvern shrugged. "No idea. Black cloth of some sort."

"Ah, well, if you don't need them, we could put the cloth to use. Nothing goes to waste in this house. Perhaps you would send them over with the newspapers next time."

Bertie nearly choked. She glanced furtively at Elizabeth and cleared her throat. "What I meant to say is, none of the neighbors appear to be afraid."

"I see your point." Mulvern rubbed his jaw. "Somebody had to see something. Fact of the matter is, they're all deuced tight-lipped. I've heard rumors. And just this morning, I noticed Turner laying on new thatch. I'll wager the French rascal left him one of those famous bags of coins I've heard the servants whispering about."

"How lovely!" Lavinnia sighed happily and held up a piece of velvet cloth she was working on. "Mrs. Turner is about to have another wee one. New thatch will keep them warmer and dryer next winter." She smiled her approval on the group.

Lord Mulvern looked outraged at her suggestion. "Ain't lovely! It's thievery! Sir Godfrey's money. Not theirs."

Lavinnia dropped her sewing into her lap and lowered her head.

He calmed down and moderated his tone. "Of course, Turner won't say how he got the coin. But, it had to be one of those confounded velvet bags."

Nana Rose clucked her tongue. "Ought to have been *your coin*, Adrian, thatching that roof. He's your tenant. Their youngest almost died from the cold last winter. Unless, perhaps, you think you can stand the weight of another death on your soul."

"Don't start with me, Rose." Lord Mulvern flexed his jaw. "Look about you. This is practically a widows and orphans' home I'm funding here. Spending every spare penny I have to take care of your lot. Why I stand the expense is more than I can fathom. It isn't enough I'm bankrolling every poor relation in my brother's family, but you must go and give refuge to every destitute female for miles around."

"You're the soul of generosity, and we're grateful." Lavinnia smiled admiringly at him. "You have a good heart, Adrian."

Nana Rose coughed forcedly and grumbled under her breath. "A guilty heart. Trying to stave off roasting in hell for his crimes."

"Refreshments, Lord Mulvern? Trace?" Elizabeth quickly got up, grabbed the bell from her grandmother's side table, and rang it perhaps a little louder than she needed to.

The maid appeared in the doorway.

"Food and drink, Maggie, for the gentlemen."

The maid whispered to Elizabeth, but in the silence surely everyone overheard. "What would you have me bring, milady? The biscuits is gone. And we used the last of—"

"*Surely,* you and Cook can think of something." Elizabeth sat back down and attempted to take the reins of the conversation firmly in hand. She turned to Trace. "How do you plan to capture these highwaymen?"

"The first—"

Mulvern interrupted. "That's why we've come. The tenants are as closemouthed as a passel of black-robed monks. I want the truth from you. Have those scoundrels left you money?"

Elizabeth averted her eyes. "Money?"

"Don't play coy with me, my girl. Fabric don't come cheap." He picked up a corner of the velvet lying in Lavinnia's lap. "Yet, here you all are, sewing."

"Well, I'm not." Bertie thrummed her fingernails against the wooden arm of her chair.

Mulvern ignored her. "Speak up, Lizzy. Did you receive money from the thieves?"

She opened her palm. The appropriate answer eluded her like a butterfly. "It's possible."

She glanced at Trace. He sat on the rickety

chair, alert, studying her, studying the room. All too observant.

She capitulated quickly, the lie souring her mouth, but there was no help for it. "Very well. Yes. We received a few coins. A small bag left on the porch. Enough for some fabric, but that is all. It could have been from anyone. Perhaps someone in the village felt charitable. As you said, many girls with nowhere to go come here—"

Mulvern slapped his hands on the frayed settee, flecks of aged horsehair puffed up around his fingers. "Betrayed by my own kin! You see!" He waved his hand through the air indicting the inhabitants of the Dower House, serving up his plight to Trace. "Even *they* are in collusion with the robbers."

The corner of Trace's mouth curved upward. "Clever, our robbers. Very clever. They ingratiate themselves with the whole neighborhood, thus protecting any information that may lead to their capture."

"Aye, and what are we to do about it?"

Trace rubbed his jaw thoughtfully. "I suggest, my lord, that you set a snare. Hold a ball. Order cakes and pastries from the village, just as you normally would for one of your dinner parties. Buy meats from the butcher. Cut flowers. Hire local musicians."

"A ball! Deuced expensive. And for what? So that my guests may be waylaid en route? I think not." Mulvern crossed his arms stubbornly.

Lizzy admired the eager gleam in Trace's eyes. A man ready for the hunt. He would be a formidable opponent.

"Ah, but that's the beauty of it." He leaned forward, advancing his idea, pausing until he held all of their attention captive. "You will not invite any guests. A *false* ball, if you will, to lure out our French rascal. The rogue is bound to hear of all the preparations. Such a night would be more temptation than he and his band can resist."

Lord Mulvern scratched at his wiry side whiskers as he considered.

Elizabeth could not resist tampering with Trace's scheme. She tilted her head sideways. "Ah, I see. So, you will lay a trap. Perhaps a coach filled with men, guns primed and at the ready?"

Trace smiled approvingly. "Always the quick mind, Lizzy. Yes. That's it, exactly."

She tapped a finger against her cheek. "A shame to waste all that food for no guests. Not to mention the cost of musicians." She poised on the edge of the settee. "What if your French highwayman should peek into Lord Mulvern's windows? Will he not smell out the ruse?"

Mulvern grunted. "All the better. I'll post men to keep watch on the grounds. Blow the fellow into the next realm if he steps foot on m'place."

"Oh." She nodded, and then sighed heavily. "Unfortunately, you might accidentally shoot one of the children from the village merely coming to spy on your wonderful ball. You know how they love to see the adults dancing and dressed in their finery."

Nana Rose sniffed. "What's one more death to his credit, among so many?"

Lord Mulvern exhaled loudly and frowned at his former sister-in-law.

Lavinnia mewed. "I can understand the children's curiosity." Her round little shoulders lifted eagerly. "I would like to peek at it myself. A ball would be perfectly splendid. Haven't been to a ball this age. I know the twins would adore it."

Mulvern shifted uneasily.

Elizabeth could scarcely keep from smiling.

Trace sat, arms folded, with that all-too-observant look on his face again.

Time to bring the game to a close, Elizabeth decided. "Perhaps it would aid your ruse if we filled out the guest list? There are quite a number of us. We might lend credence to the appearance of a ball."

"Oh yes!" Bonnie jumped up, toppling the stool. "How wonderful it would be to eat cakes and meat. Any meat, aside from rabbit. Do you think you'll serve roast beef, Uncle Adrian? Oh, that would be heavenly."

Lord Mulvern sank back, somewhat colored in his cheeks. "Yes. Fine. We'll make it a family affair, eh?"

"How lovely." Lavinnia's pleasure shifted to alarm. "Oh, but what will we wear? The girls have nothing at all."

Lord Mulvern ran a finger around his collar. "It's a *false* ball. No sense fussing overmuch with your appearance."

Trace grinned sideways at Elizabeth. "It might perfect the illusion if the ladies were dressed properly. I believe, my lord, you still have a closet full of my mother's dresses, do you not? Perhaps the ladies might make over some of those to suit the occasion?"

Lord Mulvern looked down, a blanket of sadness thrown over his features. He mumbled and shook his head. "Dora's. . . . .they were . . . hers."

Nana Rose looked at Elizabeth. Elizabeth glanced covertly at Lavinnia. The three of them knew from personal experience the anguish underneath Lord Mulvern's hesitancy.

Lavinnia covered his hand with hers. "Never you mind, Adrian. We will make do. You keep those dresses just as they were."

"No." Mulvern sighed. "I suppose it would be better to put them to good use. I'll send over the gowns. Should have done so long ago."

Nana Rose tilted her head and squinted at him, curiously.

The maid interrupted, setting a teapot and two chipped cups and saucers down by the accounting book on the table. Elizabeth slipped the book away, tucking it under the settee. She lifted the teapot lid and grimaced. It was half full with weak tea. She poured, setting a cup before each gentleman.

Trace thanked her graciously and managed to balance on the rickety chair and drink the pitiful concoction as if perfectly at ease.

Lord Mulvern took one look at the liquid in his cup and set the cup back on the saucer. "We must be going. I want to interview more of the tenants. I mean to discover exactly who's been receiving booty from the thieves."

Bertie snorted. "Won't say a word with you there, now will they?"

"Bertie is right." Trace set his cup down. "A fruitless venture."

Elizabeth spoke, quietly, uncertain of the wisdom behind her offer. "I'm to deliver sick-baskets for the vicar tomorrow. Perhaps I might ask if anyone has seen anything, and then report back to you."

Lord Mulvern brightened. "She's onto something there."

Trace agreed and asked if he might accompany her.

Mulvern's interest heightened. "Aye, and have a look about while Lizzy is talking to them. Bound to be a clue of some sort. Someone must've helped the wounded fellow. Godfrey said the blighter shrieked like a banshee. Had to have been shot well and good."

Bonnie clapped her hands together. "Perhaps they buried the bandit in the woods. Maybe you should search for a fresh grave."

Mulvern frowned at Bonnie. "Morbid speculation for a gel."

Lizzy hurried to cover her cousin's faux pas. "We've been lax in her choice of books—too many gothic novels, I'm afraid."

Mulvern tapped his fingers on his thighs. "On the other hand, she might be on to something. I ought to have some men comb the woods."

Elizabeth glared at Bonnie.

The minx waggled her shoulders back and forth, like a smug child who knows a secret. "I don't know what good it will do. Rained yesterday. A grave would be washed out. Wolves would have ripped apart the carcass and chewed the bones to pieces."

Mulvern grimaced. "Egad, child. How ghoulish! Yes, by all means, you must restrict her reading." He sniffed and straightened the lace at his cuff. "Aside from that, there haven't been wolves in that forest for a hundred years."

Bonnie shrugged. "Even if wolves didn't eat it, other scavengers would."

Blythe sat silently in the background, hiding behind her silken hair.

Elizabeth decided there had been enough precarious discussions for one afternoon. "Blythe, dear, will you play something for us?"

Without answering, Blythe turned to the pianoforte, her fingers moving over the keyboard with clarity and passion. In some passages she played the keys so softly the hammers barely struck the strings, and at other times, with such ferocity that the old pianoforte fairly thundered.

Everyone listened, barely breathing, as she filled their minds with exotic cadences and images of midnight dancing among the trees of Claegburn Wood. The sewing lay forgotten in their laps, and even restless Bertie did not move until Blythe struck the last note.

The room lay still, except for the ticking of the old clock on the cupboard. Trace inhaled deeply and glanced at Elizabeth, his brows raised. "She's talented." He leaned forward addressing Blythe. "That was beautiful. Enchanting. Was it a sonata perhaps? What is the name of the piece?"

She startled everyone by looking up, her pale blue eyes boring directly into his. "I call it, *The Highwayman's Rhapsody.*"

Trace recoiled, resting against the back of the decrepit chair, his brows pinched together. Calculating. Elizabeth panicked. She remembered from their youth that intense look in his eyes. Saw his mind leaping to solve the puzzle. He was far too quick to be toyed with in this manner. They were all foolishly underestimating him.

She sprang up, thanking the gentlemen for their visit.

Unhurriedly, Trace rose, hat in hand, brushing

away some invisible lint from the crown. He stood beside her shoulder, suddenly inscrutable, and quietly quizzed her. "Tell me Lizzy, do you still play chess?"

She looked up, surprised that he'd remembered. "Not since our last game."

"Ah, then we must have a rematch. I can't recall who won the last time?"

"Gudgeon. You know full well, I did."

The corner of his mouth curved up speculatively. "Did you? I could have sworn it was I."

Chapter 3

Bonnie squealed with delight when she saw the gowns Trace brought with him.

Elizabeth frowned at her young cousin's exuberance, but there was no repressing Bonnie.

The girl whirled around with a lovely pink silk dress hugged to her chest. "Oh, look, Lizzy! Is it not the most beautiful thing you have ever seen?" An instant later, her joy transferred to a pale blue damask, which she held up to Blythe. "This one is perfect for you." She dragged her sister to the mirror in the hallway and demanded her twin concede the statement.

Elizabeth touched Trace's arm. "Thank you for bringing the gowns so quickly. They could talk of nothing else last night."

"You'll need to alter them quickly. Lord Mulvern plans to hold the ball as soon as possible. He has already sent to London for musicians. Oh, that reminds me." He pulled a small note from his chest pocket. "He sent this. For Lavinnia. An invitation, I believe, to help him decide upon the menu."

Elizabeth arched her brow in mock awe. "An invitation to the manor. I daresay Aunt Lavinnia will be in alt. We will have to pull her down from the ceiling."

"He means well, Lizzy. Always did far better by me than duty required. Just a bit preoccupied sometimes. Ever since mother—"

"I didn't mean . . ." She laid the note by the clock.

"I know." Trace turned to the stack of remaining dresses. "Which of these will you choose?" He lifted the edge of one of the gowns, briefly caressing the soft silk between his thumb and forefinger. "I thought this gold, against your dark hair. But, I see, you look very well in purple."

"Thank you." Elizabeth glanced down at her best dress, a plain, violet mourning gown. She had covered the worn hem with a darker purple ruffle and put a bow of the same color on each of the sleeves. This morning, she'd fiddled for far too long on her stubborn hair, trying to pin it up in loose curls. It probably looked more like a jumble of flapping crow's wings than anything else. *Foolishness.*

She turned to the business at hand. "The vicar only sent two baskets today. Shall we be on our way?"

The day was fine and clear, birds twittered happily, and only a few white clouds dawdled in the blue sky. Trace helped Elizabeth step up into Lord Mulvern's dogcart, pulled by a beast far superior to the ladies' tired old nag.

"This will be a rare treat. Daffodil, our mare, only trots under threat of death. Poor old thing."

Trace settled himself beside her. She could not help but breathe in deeply, shaving soap and boot black, brushed wool and starched linen, a dozen tiny tantalizing scents completely foreign in a house full of women.

He flicked the reins and the cart rolled briskly away from the Dower House. "How bad is it?" he asked.

The question startled her. "What? How bad is what?"

"I'm not blind, Lizzy. You must tell me. How far has Mulvern's parsimony stretched? I will speak to my stepfather. Do you have enough to eat?"

Her hand lifted as if she were going to make a point and then dropped into her lap. "We get along well enough."

"Oh yes. So I see. Marvelous tea yesterday. Not everyone can afford such lavish—"

"Yes, well, it is not entirely his fault. He and Nana Rose are forever carping at one another. You may have forgotten."

"Ah, let me see if I recall." He pinched his mouth into the exact prune shape Nana Rose liked to use. "Not since Cain slew Abel, and Joseph's brothers threw him down the well, has a brother behaved so brutally . . ."

She laughed. "You do remember."

He steered adroitly around a puddle of rainwater. "Of course, I remember. It is you who are forgetful."

She sensed he was setting a trap. A gentle breeze blew pleasantly against her face before she answered. "I? What have I forgotten?"

"Promises."

Her stomach twisted uncomfortably.

An officer in command, he laid the charge directly to her. "Why did you not answer my letters?"

Why? Because it would hurt too much if you never came back. Because dashed hopes are worse than no hope. Or, at least, she had thought so. "I did write."

"Oh yes." He nodded sternly. "One letter, Lizzy. One letter."

She looked away, out into the trees.

He pulled a folded page of parchment from his pocket and set it on her lap. "One letter to warm a man's heart through all the trying nights of war. Here. Perhaps you would like to read over your masterpiece."

She rubbed her thumb against the worn edges of the folded letter. She didn't have to read it. She knew the paltry sums included there. Just as Sir Godfrey had hidden his real purse, so Elizabeth had hidden her true thoughts, years ago, and handed Trace false words. Bland watery words, like weak unsalted soup. It pricked at her conscience, as sharply as if Trace held her at sword point. "I didn't think you would come back."

"What? And these were the sentiments you sent a dying man?"

"No!" She crumpled the letter. "Not that. I never thought you would be killed. I couldn't bear to think that. I didn't believe you would ever come back *here*. To Claegburn." *To me. I thought you would break my heart. As if, when you left, the wretched thing didn't shatter anyway.* "Uncle Adrian said you might aspire to great things. You had a brilliant future." *A future that didn't include me.*

Trace held out his palm. "My letter."

She looked down at the wrinkled folds of paper in her lap, a humiliating testament to her stingy soul. "I would rather you didn't keep it."

He took it away from her and stuffed it back in his pocket.

They rode in silence to the Turners' hut. Elizabeth climbed down from the gig before he could help her. She carried the basket, making sure the small bag of coins was tucked securely under a loaf of bread.

A little girl ran out, barefoot, and clad in a plain white shift in dire need of laundering. "Wady Whizzabess! What has you brung us?"

Behind her straggled Mrs. Turner, belly round as a melon, a lock of hair stringing down across her cheek, and a small boy clinging to one leg.

Elizabeth looped the basket through one arm and scooped up the eager toddler. "Good morning, Miss Mary." She smiled and tucked some of Mary's wild curls behind the child's tiny ears. "I've brought you fresh bread, and sausages, and lots of other delicious things from the ladies in the village. How is your mother today?"

Mrs. Turner chuckled from the doorway. "As well as can be, with one babe about to spring out and another one still wrapped around my leg. Tom is in the fields, but he'll be back midday. Come in." She glanced quizzically at Trace. Elizabeth performed the introductions.

The hut was small and dark. When Trace ducked under the lintel and entered, there seemed very little room left. Obviously, he would find no sign of the highwaymen here, only a cramped room, children in need of bathing, and a bench in the midst of repair.

"I'll finish this, shall I?" He took the rough-hewn leg and worked it into the vacant opening on the bench. As she unpacked the sausages and chatted with Mrs. Turner, Elizabeth watched him covertly. He went out and dipped a cup into the rain barrel, and then returned to trickle water around the edge of the joint. When the water penetrated the wood of the leg, it would swell, causing it to stay firmly in place.

She and Trace stayed only a short while, time enough for Elizabeth to finish unloading the basket, discreetly hide the velvet bag behind the salt in Mrs. Turner's cupboard, and hand Mary a bright yellow lemon drop.

When they left, Trace turned north down the road through Claegburn Wood.

Elizabeth shook her head. "The Bernard farm is in the other direction."

"A small detour."

"Through Claegburn Wood?"

He smiled. "So, you haven't entirely forgotten."

She said nothing, as the dogcart meandered deeper into the forest of beech trees with thickly twisted trunks and tall birches, creaking and bending in the slight breeze, leaves shivering and catching the sun like green-gold guineas.

"It hasn't changed much. Still beautiful." He glanced sidelong at her as if he included her in the compliment.

She took a deep breath. He didn't belong here. These were her woods now. He was a trespasser.

He spoke as casually as if they were sitting in the Dower House parlor. "Sir Godfrey told my father he heard music the night they were robbed. A flute, or so he thought."

Or was it casual conversation? She glanced at him. "A flute? How odd. Perhaps it was his imagination. This is one of the old places. People are afraid druid spirits still roam these woods. It was dark. And you know how the wind whistles through the trees." *Thou doth protest too much.* Elizabeth clamped her lips together.

"Yes." He answered slowly, pensively, watching

her carefully. "Those were my very thoughts, until I heard Blythe play that haunting melody yesterday, a tune very much like the one Godfrey described."

Elizabeth fought to moderate her breathing. "What can you mean? How can someone truly describe one tune enough to set it apart from another? It must be heard."

He shrugged, as if it were nothing. "Perhaps she plays the flute at night in the woods."

"Nana Rose would never allow such a thing."

He laughed to himself. "It wouldn't be the first time a young girl slipped out of the Dower House to play in the woods at night."

She took in a quick breath. "I . . . that was different."

"Was it?" He turned the rig down a small path, overgrown from lack of traffic. "She might be meeting someone. A rendezvous."

"With highwaymen? Bandits? I think not!"

"Perhaps with only one bandit."

"No. Never. Blythe is not that sort of child. She would never—I know what you are thinking. But she is not like me, not nearly so reckless, or so foolish."

He stopped the dogcart by a tree. *Their tree.* Oh, she knew every tangled branch of that old beech by heart. Boughs that had begun as separate fingers of the same root, stretched upward seeking the light, twisting and coiling around one another until they all melded together to form one thick fantastic trunk.

Trace jumped down from the driver's bench and came for her, holding her too long as he lifted her down. "I promised I'd come back, Lizzy."

He didn't wait for an answer, but clasped her hand, pulling her beside him toward the trunk of their tree, until they stood face to face, as they had so many years ago. He pressed her palm flat against the smooth white bark and covered it with his. "We promised. You should have believed me."

The ancient beech bark was the color of ashes burnt to whiteness, spent and dry, the color of her dreams. She slid her hand out from under his. "A child's promise. We were children."

"We were friends."

Yes. Friends. They'd been that. Amidst all the turmoil, clinging to their games and secret places, as if the ravages of death did not exist in these woods. "Companions in sorrow."

"More than that." His gaze pierced her through.

She felt the need to run away and hide, like the game they had played as children. "You went away." Her accusing tone sounded harsher than she would have wished.

"To school. I had no choice. But at harvest-time, before my commission, do you not remember?"

Remember? Was he mad? She might try to forget. But, Lucifer and all his demons would torment her eternally with the memory of that one luminous moment. One kiss that still scorched her soul. A kiss that meant everything, and then nothing, turning her heart to ash when she heard the truth behind its melting urgency. He was leaving. Going to war. She would only ever have that one kiss. "You left. Again."

"I said I'd come back. And you promised—"

"That was four years ago, Trace." She turned away from him, leaning her forehead against the cool bark.

"You didn't believe me."

"Should I have? At one and twenty, I was already on the shelf. Most women that age are married and have children. You left. You went away to build a life without me. Don't chide me for not waiting here under this wretched tree."

"I wrote to you. We were friends. I thought someday . . ."

"Someday?" She laughed softly. "*Someday* is a Banbury tale told to lull children to sleep. You cast off Claegburn and all its grief. I couldn't fault you. If I'd been a man, I'd have done the same."

He toyed with the obstinate hairs at the base of her neck. "When you didn't write, I thought, perhaps, you'd met someone else."

She closed her eyes, pressing her head harder against the smooth bark, as if the old beech might hold the comfort of a mother's shoulder. "No. I've said my last prayers, Trace. I have my family to care for. The twins are the closest thing to children I will ever—"

"Lizzy, don't be foolish." He stroked the sides of her shoulders as if trying to warm away her cold thoughts. "You're still vibrant and even more lovely than—"

"Don't." She spun, to face him. "I heard all about the camp followers and the beautiful women in Spain."

He pressed his hands against the trunk beside her head, trapping her, bearing down on her. "I'm a man of my word, Lizzy. The intrigues of Napoleon's strategy occupied my nights, and the lives of my men consumed my days. You should have written."

His mouth was a pawn's length from hers. She held her breath, unmoving. Afraid to hope. Afraid not to hope. Heaven above! Where was her sword when she needed it? She might hold him hostage, extract everything she desired from him, lost words, missed touches. She would rob him of every kiss he owned, if only she had her sword. Instead, she was his hostage. Held captive by lips, his intoxicatingly masculine smell, and wicked blue eyes that made long dead flames burn again.

His lips moved in a husky whisper. "I believe I will collect, now."

"Collect?" She gulped air, breaking the simple word into too many throaty syllables. Heat crawled up her neck and blazed onto her cheeks.

"Yes." His dimples deepened. "On your part of the bargain, of course."

He did not give her a chance to debate. He covered her mouth with his, softly stealing away four years of want. She opened to him, allowing him to fill her miserly heart with warmth. And now, she would have one more memory with which Lucifer would taunt her when she made her journey through Hades.

Trace hugged her to his chest. "Lizzy, Lizzy, how I've missed you."

A tear escaped its mooring. It glided down her cheek, sliding, falling, like the last leaf of autumn. Glistening, it twirled down to crumble and rot beneath the tree, alongside the dreams that had fallen there four years ago. She'd made her choice, chosen a path that would divide them forever. Good from evil. She was a criminal. A thief. A liar. She had no future, save that which rightfully belonged to a hangman.

Sadly, gently, she pressed her hands against Trace's chest, separating them. "We have one last basket to deliver, and then I must return home. The twins ought to attend to their French lessons. Cook wants menus. The garden needs weeding."

Trace frowned, not an ordinary frown, but hard, intense, suddenly the soldier. She saw in his eyes questions roiling through his mind, questing for possible explanations. *If only he weren't such a strategist. Life is not a game. It does not come with a reliable set of rules. The knight doesn't always move two out and one over.* Trace hadn't.

And who in the blazes could ever predict what the queen would do? She climbed up into the rig and sat, hands folded primly in her lap.

Without further discussion, he maneuvered the dogcart back to the road. They delivered the basket to the Bernards, and he helped her down at the Dower House.

She was afraid to look him in the eye. "I'm sorry there weren't any signs of the Frenchman."

"Far more than you might think, Lizzy." He tipped his hat and left her standing at the door.

Chapter 4

He was not a fool. His conclusions were sound. It was the only explanation for her strange behavior. Trace stood at the corner of the bootmaker's, down the street from Mrs. Merton's boardinghouse, waiting.

He'd followed Elizabeth and Bertie as they'd made a furtive flight from the Dower House the previous evening. He'd not expected the journey to end in London. He'd expected her to lead him to the highwayman's lair in a remote dell or thicket, hiding like a beast. Clever of the blighter to hide among the congested population of London. Even as Trace reluctantly admired the Frenchman's shrewdness, he hated him for it.

His jealousy constructed a dashing enigmatic rogue out of his adversary. *He must be deuced charming to lead Lizzy astray, to command her loyalty, and her secrecy. Robin Hood be damned. The Frenchman was simply a cunning thief! He robbed women. Frightened old men. A thief! Nothing more.*

Trace was certain Lizzy would come out. She

would rendezvous with the black-hearted, French scoundrel. He was sure of it. Or, if she didn't, the unprincipled cur would come here to her. When he did, Trace would have him. And after the high-wayman danced his due on Tyburn's hanging tree, Lizzy would come to her senses.

To shield himself from the early morning drizzle, Trace pulled the collar of his greatcoat up. He would watch all day and all night if he had to. *Night.* Trace flexed his jaw muscles tight. *Just let the French devil show up at night. The hangman would not have to soil his rope.*

An hour passed. When the boardinghouse door opened, Trace prepared to dash around the corner, out of Lizzy's line of sight. But, an elderly woman emerged, crippled, assisted by a man, probably her son.

Lizzy hobbled toward Trace. She, an old crone, hunched, with a wadding hump fixed on her back, wearing miles of Nana Rose's black bombazine. From the dark depths of her poke bonnet, she watched, as the man she loved dismissed her and looked away. He didn't know her. She had half-hoped he would. Which was worse: Suffer exposure? Or be of so little consequence she was invisible? The weight of the padding on her back felt heavier and she found it easy to drag her steps.

Lizzy sighed. *Old woman. That was all he saw.* As well he should, for she *was* old. Trace deserved a young, beautiful woman, one unfettered by the bondage of her crimes, one as true and decent as he was. A heroine. Not a villain. Even so, he ought to have known her. Lizzy felt a compelling urge to rap him smartly with her cane as she shuffled past.

In a low grumbling voice, Bertie, exercising her role as attentive son, urged Lizzy forward. "Come along now, mother."

Lizzy turned back for one last glimpse. He didn't even glance in their direction. Bertie tugged forcefully on her arm. They left him standing there in the mist, guarding the boardinghouse like a faithful sentry.

When they rounded the corner, Bertie hissed, "What are you playing at, my girl? He goes by the rules, that one. If he catches us, there's no saying he won't turn us in."

"Little doubt of it." Lizzy looked straight ahead. The poke bonnet acted as a blinder, shielding her from Bertie's inspection.

"Still in love with him, aren't you?"

Elizabeth was in no mood to pretend it wasn't so, or to ask foolish questions such as, *How did you know?* She shrugged. "What does it matter? It's impossible."

"Folderol."

"I'm too old."

"Balderdash."

"I'm a criminal," she whispered. "A robber. He's a war hero. He can't have a wife who deserves to go to the gallows."

Bertie shrugged. "He needn't know."

"He'd figure it out. A man like Trace can't be fooled for long. He'd uncover the truth." Lizzy tugged at the black silk. "About this. About all of it. He'd know I deceived him."

"May find out anyway."

"Not if we're careful."

"Look here, Elizabeth." Bertie halted their progress and turned to face her. "I disagree. He's a first-rate fellow. If you want him, we'll all keep mum. No one need ever know about . . . the business."

"Lies? Between husband and wife? It wouldn't be the honorable thing." *Honorable?* The irony choked her. She laughed, one dismal shudder. "Even if I could keep it from him, I'd live every day of my life wondering if, and when, the sword might fall."

Bertie blew out a ruff of air letting her lips ripple loudly. "Then there's no way round it. It's a gamble, but you'll have to tell him the truth, straightaway."

Elizabeth inhaled deeply. Hadn't she toyed with that very idea 900 times? "No point. I know him. He couldn't stomach it. And I couldn't bear to see the look of disgust in his eyes. I'd rather hang."

Bertie didn't say anything more. It was one of the things Lizzy loved about Bertie: she knew when to be quiet. They walked the rest of the way to the jeweler's shop in silence.

The jeweler set his lens down on the black velvet cloth and shook his head. "A shame they aren't still in their original setting. Diamonds of this mediocre quality are worth far more mounted."

Bertie snarled low in her throat. "It was the only way my mother could get them out of France. In their settings, they're far too difficult to hide. Surely you must know this, yes?"

"Yes. Yes. Of course." The jeweler waved his hand dismissing the argument. "It is the same story with all the French émigrés. But what can I say?"

"How much?" Bertie demanded.

"One hundred pounds."

"Robbery, sir!"

"It is the going rate."

Lizzy spat out a string of vehement French oaths to Bertie, who nodded and turned back to the jeweler. "She says, she did not escape Madam Guillotine and her band of scurrilous swine to come here and have an Englishman cut her throat. Make a better offer, or we will go elsewhere."

"One hundred and thirty. That is my final bid." He folded his arms stubbornly.

Lizzy brusquely moved aside the jeweler's glass, gathered up the edges of the velvet, and tied a cord around the glittering pile of Sir Godfrey's wife's dismantled diamonds. She deposited the small bag into the recesses of her black bombazine and shuffled out of the store.

Their experience at the next jeweler's shop was only a moderate improvement. They trudged back to the boardinghouse, discouraged.

"Two hundred pounds." Lizzy lamented. "I had thought five hundred, at the very least."

"Skinflints. Miserly old gets. They'll sell those diamonds for three times that."

"Undoubtedly."

"What's the tally? Will we have enough to bring the twins out next season?"

"Not nearly. It was going to be a scrape even if we'd gotten the five hundred."

"Could just bring out Bonnie."

"No! We agreed. Neither of them should have to molder away without a future. Blythe deserves a husband and children as much as Bonnie does. She may be quiet, but she still has the heart of a woman. She needs—"

"Very well." Bertie put up her hand to stem Lizzy's impassioned arguments. "You've no complaint from me. One more midnight tryst should do it."

No complaint, indeed. Lizzy frowned. Bertie's tone reflected altogether too much enthusiasm. "I don't like it. Not with Trace on the hunt." Lizzy inhaled deeply. "If only there was another way."

"Fiddle-faddle. More of a challenge. Half the fun is the game."

"Think of the risk. Not just for us, but the twins."

"Leave them out of it, then. It'll be just the two of us. Better sport for us."

"Excessively difficult to deal with outriders with only two of us. Aside from that, if we're caught, the scandal alone would ruin Blythe and Bonnie's lives."

"Won't get caught."

"You underestimate Trace. He's tenacious. Thorough." Lizzy gestured toward the corner where he still stood guard on the boardinghouse. "Observe. He's still there."

Bertie chuckled. "I daresay he'll stand there all night."

"In this rain? What if he catches pneumonia? I won't have that preying on my conscience as well. The sooner we leave, the sooner he'll go home, out of this merciless drizzle."

"Think, Lizzy. If we come to London and go nowhere, what will he deduce?"

She sighed. "He might figure it out."

"Just so."

Elizabeth nodded. "We'd best do some shopping. Feathers for Nana Rose. Perhaps a fan for Lavinnia."

"Heard of a confectioner . . ." Bertie hesitated, a childlike expression lighting her aged features. "I would dearly love to try one of those new—"

"Ices from Gunter's." Lizzy beamed.

"Precisely."

Trace rubbed at his neck, which was growing stiff from craning to watch the doorway down the road. He noted the elderly woman and her son returning to the boardinghouse. Still no sign of Lizzy. It wasn't like her to be a slug-a-bed. Where was she? Had the blasted Frenchman slipped past him somehow?

He was rewarded twenty minutes later. Elizabeth and Bertie walked out, opening a broad black umbrella, chatting like young girls, as carefree as pigeons in the King's park. He followed them to Piccadilly Street.

Admirable, Lizzy thought, how he followed at a distance, trying to blend in with the crowd, collar up, hat low. She and Bertie went, first, to dicker with merchants over paste pearls for Blythe and Bonnie. Next, they went down the street to bargain for a silk fan for Lavinnia and a pair of frothy ostrich feathers for Nana.

He was skilled at concealing himself, but it was impossible for a man of Trace's stature and bearing to remain completely hidden. He may have dressed like every other man on the street, but his walk exuded authority. She knew where he was almost without looking. She could feel his presence and longed to draw near, but couldn't.

They strolled to Berkley Square for ices. Saddest of all was catching sight of him outside the window at Gunter's, his coat rain-soaked and his hat sodden. She hated that he should be out there in the murk, while they indulged in the delicious, sweet, lemony treat from inside the comfortable shop. "This is absurd. We should invite him in."

Bertie waved her spoon indecorously at Lizzy. "Can't do it, my dear. Smash his male sensibilities to bits if he knew you'd spotted his game."

"He would adore this lemon ice. It's heavenly." Lizzy spooned up some of the delectable mixture.

"Let him see you enjoying it." Bertie laughed. "Serves him right for being so clever."

Chapter 5

The Dower House overflowed with happy jab-
ber and sighs of delight, as the women readied
themselves for the false ball.

"You look magnificent, Nana." It was the first time
in Lizzy's memory her grandmother had donned
anything other than widow's garb.

Lord Mulvern hadn't sent a gown for Nana
Rose, to which the grand dowager had snapped, "I
don't need *his* charity. I have a perfectly good
wardrobe of my own."

Indeed, her gown was a Georgian masterpiece,
a full skirt with panniers of deep blue figured silk
and a silver lace paneled front. With her white hair
piled high, she looked like a queen from times
past, albeit a queen without any jewelry.

Elizabeth was the last to ready herself. The candles on her dressing table fluttered as she slid the
gold sarcenet gown over her head. She watched in
the mirror as the soft golden fabric shimmered
gracefully, falling with feather light caresses over
her breasts and hips, draping the curves of her

body in spiderweb thin silk. The slippery fabric teased at her flesh, flaring the hunger that had been steadily mounting since the day Trace had taken her to Claegburn Wood.

He had kept his distance since that day. Wise choice. Always so disciplined, Trace. She, on the other hand, had been left to the mercy of her lurid imagination, that impish portion of her vile brain, relentless in its wicked desire to drive her mad with unattainable cravings.

For this one night, she would pretend she was an alluring princess, a woman free to follow her heart. A seductress. He would pay for making her want him again.

"Helen of Troy." Blythe stood in the doorway. "She looked liked you."

"That's very kind of you to say." Elizabeth smiled. "Would you help me with these ties, dearest?"

Thin ropes of gold crisscrossed Grecian-style over Lizzy's breasts. Blythe deftly wound the cords over the fabric and tied them in back, murmuring as she worked. "Troy fell. Greeks plundered the city. Paris was slain. Hecabe howled in grief."

Perhaps it had not been a compliment, after all. "Are you worried about this evening, Blythe?"

"Grandmother made pockets. Bertie's reticule is too big. It's a Trojan horse."

Unfounded fears? Anxiety? Or could it be that Blythe was the only one in the house with any sense? Trace's parting words echoed in Lizzy's ears. He had guessed something, but what? Followed them to London, but why? Were they in danger? Perhaps, but not tonight.

"Blythe, darling, you're right. There is a Trojan horse tonight. That must be what you are sensing. It will be outside. A coach, full of armed men, sent to flush out the highwaymen. They will be out on the roads, riding up and down, hoping to snare us. But we will be having a lovely time dining at Lord Mulvern's table and listening to music. Do you see?"

Blythe lowered her eyes. Lizzy hugged her. "All will be well. I promise."

Lord Mulvern's coach arrived to collect the ladies of the Dower House. It was impossible to squeeze all six of them into the carriage.

"Do try to scoot over a little farther, Rose." Lavinnia wriggled herself onto the seat next to her mother-in-law. Nana Rose's hoops bulged up so high that Lavinnia was almost hidden behind them. "If you will, kindly pull the cord, and bunch up your panniers?"

Grandmother remained posed primly on the seat, her white pompadour wedged against the ceiling and her ostrich feathers bowed over. She did not budge an inch. "The hinge is broke."

"It won't do." Bertie stood outside the door, her arms folded stubbornly. "Too cramped. Can't breath in there. Enough flower scent to suffocate a bee-hive."

Nana Rose scowled at her daughter. "Don't be ridiculous. You can't ride on the roof."

"Can and will." Bertie pulled up the hood of her cape and turned to the footman. "Don't stand there like a jackass. Help me up onto the box."

Without displaying even the slightest inkling of astonishment, the very proper footman aided and abetted the recalcitrant Bertie, who was bound to be a great deal more comfortable on the driver's seat beside a scandalized coachman than crammed into the coach with the rest of them. Fortunately, it was a short journey to Lord Mulvern's home.

Elizabeth hadn't been back to Claegburn Manor in many months. The house always brought back a flood of memories from when she and her parents had lived there, when her father had been Lord Mulvern.

Each of the women, except the twins, remembered their sojourn in the house. Better not to think of those days. Yet, how could they not? The very sound of their feet on the marble, the curve of the staircase, the quality of light glittering from the chandelier—every small detail evoked images from days long lost. Fathers, brothers, sons . . . these women also keenly recalled the Claegburn men, who had sojourned there with them.

Elizabeth could still see her mother smiling at her from the drawing room, her father standing by his study door at the end of the hallway. Trace running down the stairs, his mother reprimanding him for his haste. Ghosts, all. Save one.

Would he be here tonight? Or, was Trace out riding with the ruse coach, waiting to ambush and capture the Frenchman and his band of rogues? She hoped not. She had an ambush of her own planned, schemes and traps, a dozen little torments she intended to practice on him. Let him discover the anguish of wanting something, someone, beyond his reach.

Bonnie, who had no weighty memories dragging at her feet, pattered gaily up the stairs, close behind the butler, leading the way up to the dining room. Elizabeth quietly reminded her cousin that Nana Rose must enter first.

The butler announced with a flourish, "The Dowager Lady Mulvern."

Nana Rose paraded into the ballroom, head erect, a bittersweet mask hiding the turmoil Lizzy knew her grandmother must feel to be announced as a guest in what had been her own home.

Bonnie leaned forward and peeked around the doorjamb, giggling at her grandmother's stately entrance. Lizzy nudged the pink minx and sent her a silent scold. The girl must learn to watch her manners before they took her to London for a season.

The butler announced Lavinnia, who strode amiably into the room. Shorter than Trace's mother had been, Lavinnia had cleverly altered the green silk gown, giving it an elegant train.

Lizzy would like to have seen Lord Mulvern's face when he saw Lavinnia. From the hallway, they heard his gruff voice ring out satisfyingly. "Lavinnia! 'Pon my word, you look quite handsome."

Bonnie hid her mirth behind her hand, her golden curls jounced in adorable perfection. She would do well in London, even without much of a dowry. Bonnie, at least, would not spend her life a spinster, as Elizabeth and Bertie would do. Neither would Blythe, if Lizzy had anything to do with it.

Blythe looked like a fairy princess captured from Claegburn Wood and dragged into the light against her will. Beautiful, but desirous of escape.

"You needn't worry," Lizzy whispered, trying to reassure her.

"Lady Bertilde Claegburn," the butler called. Bertie squared her shoulders and marched into the room like a general come to inspect the troops.

Lizzy's turn next.

She floated into the ballroom, ready to snare her conquest. Candles blazed along the walls. Musicians played sedately at the far end of the room. Lord Mulvern waited, Aunt Lavinnia at his side, and another man, but not Trace.

Lizzy couldn't help it. She looked desperately around the room. Empty chairs. Familiar faces in paintings on the wall. The one face she wanted to see—missing. No Trace. Of course not, and why would he be here? To see her? Ha! He was hunting! The wretch. And she, a silly mooncalf, for thinking it would have been otherwise. She struggled to school her features.

"Thank you for inviting us, Uncle Adrian." She curtsied.

"Pleasure, Lizzy." Lord Mulvern took her hand and bowed over it graciously. "I've a surprise for you, young ladies. A dancing master." He pointed to the gentleman at his left elbow. "From London. After I hired the musicians, thought—waste of money if the gels don't know how to dance. Mr. Bledsoe, here, can show us all the latest dances, eh?"

The dancing master bowed with a flourish.

She knew how to dance. But, it was probably not the ideal time to tell Lord Mulvern that she and his stepson had practiced dancing under a midnight moon in Claegburn Wood. No, decidedly not. "That will be lovely. Most thoughtful. Thank you."

"Yes, indeed, most generous." Lavinnia smiled. "Just as I've always said."

"Tut tut, nothing to it. Shall we dine now and enjoy dancing after?"

Bonnie smiled eagerly. "By all means."

The footman threw open the doors. The magnificent dining room sparkled with silver and glass. Lord Mulvern's servants brought forth a sumptuous feast, surpassing even Bonnie's expectations. Or so, she declared, with unmuffled enthusiasm. "Beef! Oh, Uncle Adrian. It is even more delicious than I remembered."

Elizabeth toyed with the coveted roast beef, rearranging it on her plate. Disappointment filled her stomach, leaving little room for this evening's delicacies, no matter how long awaited. She glanced across the table and caught Bertie in the act of secreting a large slice of beef into her lap, probably to be shifted, just as subtly, into the "too big" reticule Blythe had mentioned. Egad! And from the satisfied gleam on Bertie's countenance, the beef was not the first item to make furtive passage to the depths of her bag.

Lizzy grimaced as more meat continued to disappear. She fervently hoped the servants were too busy to notice. During dinner, several slices of ham, a loaf of cheese, three apples, four dried spiced pears, and a half-dozen sculptured sugar confections found their way to Bertie's pantry under the table.

When, at last, dinner ended and they left the dining room, Elizabeth fell in step beside Bertie. "I'm surprised you can carry your bag without assistance."

Bertie grinned, unashamed.

Lizzy inhaled her chagrin and whispered. "Good gracious. Are you not afraid it will drip?"

Bertie hefted the reticule. "I lined it with oil cloth. Tight as a ship."

Another rather odd-shaped ship, Nana Rose, sailed ahead of them, floating across the ballroom floor like a petite blue galleon. Nana glided directly out of the gaily-lit room to ports unknown. *She's up to something.* Lizzy started to follow her mischievous grandmother, but Bonnie waylaid her.

"Lizzy, you must come and make up our set. You and Bertie will make six. Blythe won't dance. She insists on watching the musicians."

At the far end of the room, Blythe had positioned a chair beside the trio of musicians, where she would, undoubtedly, sit and study every movement. Elizabeth dearly wished she might sit beside her young cousin and do nothing, think nothing, simply allow music to transport her to a soothing place of carefree fantasies.

Bonnie tugged her hand, pulling her into the middle of the room, where the dancing instructor led them in the steps of a *Danse Ecossoise*. It was so remarkably similar to a country-dance, Lizzy would have sworn he was making up the steps as they went along. After the vigorous romp, their instructor suggested they learn the more sedate, if rather more scandalous, steps of the waltz.

Lord Mulvern cleared his throat. "Now see here, young man! Not quite the thing for genteel young ladies."

The very elegant instructor took no affront. He mildly explained, his hand revolving gracefully as he made each of his points, that even Almack's had sanctioned the waltz. "The most elegant and fashionable balls in London boast of a waltz or even two. It is essential one know the steps, lest one appear provincial."

Lord Mulvern sputtered. "Very well. Mustn't be backward." He tried to disguise his bruised dignity and lined up beside Lavinnia. "Show us this infamous waltz."

The dancing master took a position next to Elizabeth and lifted her hand in his. At his nod, the musicians began to play in three-four time. "It is a simple square pattern, like so."

It took Elizabeth a few minutes to adapt to the correct steps. Once she did, it was a comfortable easy rhythm.

Blythe rose from her chair and stood in front of the musicians shaking her head, her hands to her ears. There was a disturbance as the fellow with the violin lost his place and stopped playing, obviously exasperated with his critic. After a whispered argument, Blythe took the instrument he thrust at her and fell in beside the other musicians.

Lizzy almost stumbled as her cousin put bow to the strings. The first strains were awkward and squawky, but in a trifling, the most beautiful sounds she had ever heard flowed from the violin. Long, deep, reverberating arpeggios arced up like a rainbow to meet quick high staccato chords. The waltz took on a new character, one full of passion.

As the dancing master led Elizabeth in a turn, completing the square pattern, she nearly lost her breath. He stood in the doorway. His gaze fixed on her. Trace!

He strode into the room, halted Lord Mulvern's waltz with Lavinnia, and whispered in his stepfather's ear. Lord Mulvern nodded gravely and turned back to find his step with Lavinnia.

Music echoed around the nearly empty ballroom. Yet, she heard each of Trace's footfalls report on the wood floor, marked each footstep coming closer, growing louder, until at last, he stopped at her side. He tapped the dancing master's shoulder. "If I may?"

The dancing master bowed without a word and handed Lizzy into Trace's arms.

She smiled, pleased beyond her ability to hide it. "I'm afraid, I'm not very adept at the waltz yet."

His face remained grave. Implacable. "I'm sure you will catch on quickly enough."

She felt self-conscious under his stern scrutiny. Where was the flattery she had expected? The yearning in his eyes? He spun her deftly around the room.

She tried to draw him out. "I see you've waltzed before."

"Visiting dignitaries. Military balls. Would you have expected anything less?"

Lizzy's ancestors' faces were a blur as she whirled dizzily past the paintings on the wall. He took long confident steps, waltzing her at far too vigorous a pace around the room. His chest expanded and contracted heavily, although, she guessed, it had little to do with the exertion of the dance.

As they approached the open doors to the balcony, without missing a step, he whisked her out into the darkness. The air was cool and sweet. Lord Mulvern's untended gardens were blooming profusely with spring wildflowers and gangly remnants of the garden's former glory.

Trace suited the width of his steps to the narrow balcony. The hand, which he had held with rigid correctness on her shoulder, slid lower, into the small of her back. He pulled her closer. "You didn't ask me if I caught the highwayman."

Fool! She was a fool. She'd forgotten. She'd only thought of claiming his attention. Of luring. Of tantalizing. She regulated her breathing, struggling to appear calm. "If you had, you would be jubilant, wouldn't you? Judging by your demeanor, he escaped."

"*Escaped?*" Trace laughed derisively, no humor in his eyes. "The coach went up the road. Circled round on side roads. Then came up the main road again. *And again.* Five men hired, three waiting with guns in the coach, and it goes round and round like a child's top."

He clutched her closer. The music took on a subtle quality as they moved farther away from the doors. They were almost to the edge of the balcony, where roses meandered haphazardly up the stone walls. "Tell me the truth, Lizzy."

Her feet faltered. "What do you mean?"

He caught her, supporting her in his arms, his face dangerously close. "The Frenchman. You warned him away, didn't you?"

"No." She shook her head. "I didn't. Why would you think that?"

"But, you *do* know him."

"No."

"You're lying. I see it in your eyes. I know you too well." He brushed a strand of hair out of her face, smoothing his fingers across her cheek. "You're lying. And you're afraid. But, of what? Is he your lover?"

"*Are you mad?*" She tried to pull out of his arms, but he held her in place.

"You may as well confess, Lizzy. That day in the woods, I figured it out."

"What are you saying?"

"The kiss. I knew you still loved me. I could feel it. Still feel it. The way you look at me. When I touch you . . . I can tell. But you pushed me away. There could only be one explanation. The despicable cur has some hold over you."

"No."

"Someone warned him away. I followed you to London. Did you meet him there? A rendezvous? A note passed between you? Tell me!"

"No. You don't understand." She backed up, groping for the wall, for something solid to cling to.

"Then make me understand." He grabbed her

shoulders, forcing her to look him in the eyes. "I'll believe you if you just tell me the truth."

If only she could tell him. Her anguish must have spoken too fluently. He tried to answer for her.

"Give me another explanation. You depend upon the money he leaves you? Has Blythe succumbed to his charm? A man like that would be a grave temptation for a young naive girl. Or did he charm you?" He stopped scrambling for an answer and searched her face.

She felt herself shaking. Desperate not to lie. Equally desperate not to be found out.

"You're shaking. I've frightened you. Forgive me, my dearest. I'm a fool. Jealousy muddled my thinking. I've gone mad wondering what you're hiding. But what was I thinking? You would never consort with a thief."

If only it were consorting. Stones on her chest, his words. She feared to breathe, but forced herself to speak, a featherlight petition that meant life or death. "What then, could you never love a thief?"

"Of course not." He almost smiled, as if she jested.

So certain his answer. Fortunately, he still held her. Her legs had no more will to do their task. She did not remember how to call the blood up from her heart, or force the air into her lungs. It no longer mattered.

"Lizzy, what's wrong?" He held her chin in his fingers. "Tell me the truth?"

I am the despicable cur, the unlovable thief.

She struggled to be free of those eyes that peered so easily into her soul. What a fool she'd been to think she could come here and pretend, even for one night, that she was worthy of his affection. "I can't."

"If he ruined you, I'll . . ."

What would you do? Kill the Frenchman? She had a mad urge to laugh. Scream. Run. Instead, all emotion drained from her, like blood from a mortal wound.

"Is that it? Hear me, Lizzy. I won't let you throw your life away for a man with no scruples, a scoundrel, a . . ." His eyes, those wretchedly earnest eyes, implored her to answer. "Give him up. Tell me the truth."

She tried to look away, but he held her tight and chased her soul. Harried, she spat what little truth she could at him, "I don't know any Frenchmen! None. Not one."

"Lizzy, please. I don't care what he's done to you. It doesn't matter. Do you hear? You belong to me. With me. You always have."

When she didn't respond, he let go and waited. A thousand miles away, inside Lord Mulvern's ballroom, the waltz played on. In the garden, crickets rasped a dull accompaniment. High above a beech tree in the woods, an owl screeched his shrill hunting cry. Silent rabbits shivered in fear.

Trace lifted a coil of her dark hair, which had fallen across her breast, and held it loosely in his fingers. "Come back to me, Elizabeth." He kissed her then, with the soft sweet sadness of one saying farewell to a dying friend.

If this was to be her last touch from him, she would have more.

Lizzy circled her arms around his neck, drawing him in, kissing him not as a corpse, but as a thief, stealing as much of his heart as he would allow.

A low rumble in his throat warned her that she'd dared too much. He pulled her against his chest, plundering her mouth, even as she ravaged his. No tender kisses. He made penetrating demands on her mouth, which meant, *these lips belong to me.* No gentle caresses. With feverish intensity, his hands lay claim to her flesh, the vaporous silk of her gown dissolved under his touch. He may as well have declared aloud, *this body belongs to me.*

Trace stopped abruptly and stepped away from her, his breath ragged. "How can you give yourself to me so freely, yet withhold the truth from me?"

She lowered her eyes. Moonlight glinted off the gold strands in her gown. "Because, the truth is far worse than you imagine."

She would never forget his face, how it looked in that moment. How the color drained, and even in the darkness he looked pale. His pain turned to outrage, and finally vengeance. She knew then, he was lost to her forever.

He backed away, pointing at her, as if he had finally identified his enemy. "Then, I *will* kill him. I swear it!"

He left her standing there, bracing herself against the wall. The perfume of roses and wild honeysuckle floated on the black breeze, like a curse. Sweetness, where there should only be bitterness. "You are too late," she whispered. "I am already dead."

Slowly, Lizzy walked back to the ballroom. As she came through the door, Nana Rose bumped into her, clinking like teacups thrown in a flour sack.

"What happened?" her grandmother demanded in a hushed voice. "I was just coming to find you.

Trace stormed through here looking as if he meant to chew a lion in half."

"Nothing. Nothing that can be helped." Lizzy took Nana Rose by the elbow and guided her toward the hallway. "Come with me to the retiring room. Do you realize you're rattling?"

"It's the hinges."

"I sincerely doubt it."

She hurried Nana into the sitting room across the hall and shut the door behind them. "Show me."

"Show you what? Are you foxed? Must have been that strong wine at dinner. You're talking nonsense."

Lizzy lifted aside one of the overskirts draping Nana's pannier. "Pockets. Very clever."

Nana Rose sniffed defensively.

Lizzy sighed. "What did you take?"

"You, of all people, ought not scold me."

"I'm not scolding."

Reluctantly, Nana Rose pulled wide the pouch hanging inside the hooped framework of her skirt.

Lizzy peeked inside and looked up, open-mouthed, at her prim and proper grandmother. "Candlesticks?"

Nana shrugged. "Silver. And I'll have you know, that snuffbox belonged to my Royce. So don't say another word about it."

"And in the other side?"

Nana grumbled but opened the other pannier for inspection.

Lizzy's shoulders sagged. "A vase? Aren't you afraid it will be in pieces by the time we get home?"

"Don't be silly. That's why I wrapped the table runner around it. Embroidered that runner myself. Only proper I should have it back."

Nana Rose picked up a tortoiseshell hairbrush.

"Do you remember this brush? Used it a hundred times during those years." She tucked the brush inside the vase.

Lizzy shook her head. "With that in there, you're bound to rattle even louder."

"Wretched entailment." Nana Rose yanked a fringed damask cover from off a small side table and packed it around the brush and vase. "*The house and all its accoutrements* . . . Men write those idiotic things. It's enough to rip a woman's heart out."

"I think, perhaps, it's time we left for the evening."

Grandmother looked longingly around the room. "Yes. Take me away, Lizzy, before I cannot walk for carrying things."

Lavinnia burst into the room, fanning herself with the new silk fan. "Waltzing. It's wonderful. Lovely. I daresay, I'm completely winded."

Nana Rose hurriedly adjusted her overskirt to hide the pockets.

Bertie strolled in behind Lavinnia, lugging her reticule. "I've had m'fill of dancing." She glanced warily from Rose to Lizzy. "Ho now, what's to do in here?"

"I'll tell you what's to do. I've exciting news." Lavinnia fanned herself, grinning like a delighted child. "Lord Mulvern is convinced the Frenchman and his band of thieves are routed. After tonight, they know they're being hunted. They won't dare risk another robbery. He's going to invite Lord Loughton and several of his old friends and their wives for a weekend of hunting and cards. And the best part is—he invited *me* to act as his hostess. Oh, we'll have music and feasting. Isn't it wonderful?"

"Perfect." Bertie's face fairly danced with predatory eagerness.

One last time and then they were done. Judging by

the excitement on Bertie's face, it might prove harder to give up their midnight trysts than Lizzy had expected.

"Wonderful. If you like that sort of thing." Nana Rose headed for the door, sagging like a weather-beaten ship. "Time we took our leave."

Late that night, after they'd gone back to the Dower House and all the Claegburn women had settled in their beds, Lizzy blew out her candle and sat beside her window. She knew Trace was out there. Felt it. She strained to see into the darkness, discern shadowy shapes in the woods above the house. He would keep watch for the Frenchman, laboring under the misbegotten notion that the il-lusive highwayman would ride up to her window for a moonlit assignation.

Go to him. Her feckless heart throbbed com-mands. *Run to the woods. Find him. Tell him the truth.*

If he led her to the gallows, so be it. If he beat her for her crimes, at least he would be touching her. What good was her life without him? But, did she have the right to bring consequences down upon Bertie's head? Ruin Blythe and Bonnie's fu-ture? Shame her grandmother? Disgrace her fam-ily? She stood facing the window, her head bowed.

The moon waltzed with the dark swirling clouds. Trace leaned against a creaking birch on the rise above the Dower House. From here, no one could reach the house without his knowing. She stood in her window, taunting him, white angelic night rail, her black hair tumbling over her shoulders. He ached for her.

Come to me, Lizzy.

She must know he was here. She looked out into the forest as if she could see him. *Come out. We will waltz under the old beech. I will hold you forever, if only you come to me.*

Or, was she waiting for the Frenchman? *Devil take the bastard.* Let him show his swarthy face anywhere near Lizzy and blood would flow.

Chapter 6

Two weeks later

The midnight moon galloped high above the trees. From the rise, Trace followed the progress of Lord Loughton's borrowed coach as it turned down the secluded road into Claegburn Wood. His edgy outrider hung back, warily watching his flanks. Deeper into the thick forest the coach went, making it difficult for Trace to follow its movements.

They would strike soon, the Frenchman and his band of thugs. Trace nudged his horse down into the dense woods, hoping his mount's cautious steps would not alert the highwaymen. Through the trees, he caught glimpses of the amber coach lamps bobbing and flickering as the coach moved forward, a flash of reflected light from the harness metal, a glimmer of brass on the top rail.

A muffled cry. *The game had begun.*

Trace urged his horse to a quicker pace and approached the road. A furlong behind the coach, Trace found his fallen outrider lying in the road, thrashing about like an overgrown carp, cinched securely in a fishing net, with a rag jammed in his mouth.

Trace couldn't take the time to free his incompetent sentry. He distinguished the outline of the coach, standing still. Dismounting, Trace crept nearer, closing in on the bandits.

Only two? Where was the band of cutthroats? He'd heard tales of black-clad thieves dropping from the sky, as numerous as gutter rats, swarming over hapless coaches. Only two. He could take two by himself. One rogue in particular held his interest. The Frenchman.

Elizabeth, having dispatched the outrider, approached the coach, ready to throw open the door. Before she could reach it, the latch handle clicked and turned. The door creaked slowly open, the nostrils of a twin-barreled flintlock leading the way. Through the glass, she recognized the nervous face of one of Lord Mulvern's stablemen.

She saw it all then. Trace had beaten her at her own game. Checkmate. She slammed the carriage door against the stable lad's hand. He yipped. The pistol fell to the ground and discharged.

"Trap!" She yelled. "Run!" She scooped up the weapon and threw it into the bushes.

Footsteps thudded behind her. She turned. Black, his silhouette in the moonlight, yet she knew him. Knew he would follow her. He wanted the Frenchman. Bertie, securing the coachman, leapt down from the box and headed north, into the deep woods. Lizzy would go south, giving her aunt a chance to escape.

Like a frightened hind, she charged uphill, crashing through underbrush, dashing between trees. A thicket—she needed a thicket in which to hide. Birches sparkled white in the moonlight. The ground, a dull gray carpet of leaves. Too bright—she needed the dark of a moonless night. Treacherous silver beams slashed through the canopy of branches, illuminating the hunted.

The sound of snapping branches, whipping saplings warned her of his closeness. Night creatures scattered, pattering up trees and rustling out of their path. Her heart flapped and fluttered like a wild imprisoned bird.

The clap of gunshot alarmed her, but she was certain he had missed. A bullet would have dropped her. Surely. The fire scorching through her shoulder must have been a stab from a sharp branch. She stumbled but regained her balance and kept plowing forward. A cave. A ravine. A cleft to hide in. But there was none.

Pain spread to her lungs, making breathing an agony. She clutched her shoulder, but, through her glove, felt only the vague sensation of heat. She leaned against a sturdy beech. A copse, too dense for passage, lay ahead. Her vision blurred. *Which way? Which way?* Left, too open. Right, too steep. She needed air. Breath. The world wobbled crazily.

His boots behind her—crushing leaves, breaking sticks. He was upon her. She wheeled around in time to meet his second shot. See a tiny red spark. Hear the echoing blast.

* * *

The rogue's impertinent tricorn lay in the leaves, the feather fluttering frivolously in the wind. Let it lie there and rot. Debris. Rubbish.

Trace nudged the fallen highwayman with the toe of his boot. *It moaned.*

Intending to put the cur out of his misery, Trace aimed his pistol at the rascal's forehead. A forehead that began to look oddly familiar.

Sudden fear twisted his gut.

No! It couldn't be.

He shook his head, dropping to his knees, and ripped away the black eye mask. *"God in heaven. No!"* He yanked at the scraggy beard and discovered strings held it in place. "Lizzy! No. No. No!" Untying it, he cast the ruddy thing in the leaves.

He grabbed her shoulders and lifted her into his lap. It felt like warm clotted cream oozing over his fingers. Blood.

Trace ripped open her blouse to find the flow and stop it. A breastplate of wood, overlaid with thick tin, covered her chest. He saw then the remains of his ball lodged in the protector directly over her heart. Compulsively, he touched the indentation. At least that shot had not found its mark completely. Gray moonlight illuminated his bloody fingers. They looked black in the dim light, blood, black as sin, black as death.

He pulled her shirt off farther and found the source of the bleeding. His first shot had not missed. He snatched out his handkerchief and pressed it over the wound in her shoulder.

What had he done?

God, help her. God, help him. He couldn't live with himself if he'd killed her.

She moaned, her face as pale and ashen in the moonlight as the beech under which she lay. "Lizzy."

Her eyelids fluttered. Recognition flitted briefly in her eyes. "Take me home." She looked away. "To Nana."

He pulled off his neckcloth and wrapped it tightly around her chest and shoulder. She cried out when he lifted her up to his horse, but then lay silent in his arms as he rode to the Dower House.

Lizzy, the highwayman? A criminal? A thief. He couldn't comprehend it.

Yet, he should have guessed. All the clues were there. He should have known. London. The old woman and her son. She'd tricked him. Walked brazenly past him. Deceived him, but not in the way he'd expected. The pieces spun into place. He wanted to roar like an injured lion, howl his pain at the moon. *What a fool she must think him.*

Deceit. He hated it.

Even so, he couldn't bring himself to hate her. He looked at the stranger collapsed in his arms, the woman he thought he knew so well, but didn't know at all. She, nearly dead from his bullet. It would be so much easier if he *could* hate her. Her treachery pierced him through, as deadly as a gunshot.

Middle of the night, the Dower House should be quiet and dark. Instead, the windows flickered with candlelight. Old ladies and young women running about like it was midday. He supposed they were all in a panic. The door flew open as he rode up.

Nana Rose ran out in her night rail. "What have

you done? Is she dead? You fiend! Murderer! How could you do this? How could you kill my dear sweet girl?"

Bertie, still dressed in highwayman-black, ran out beside the old woman. "Hush, Mother. He didn't know."

The twins rushed out and stopped short at the sight of Lizzy collapsed in his arms. Nana Rose turned and clung to Bonnie, weeping.

Bertie hurried to his horse and reached for Lizzy's lifeless body, helping Trace hold her steady as he climbed down. Bertie whispered. "Is she . . . ?"

Trace shook his head. "Still breathing, but unconscious."

Females flocked around as he carried Lizzy into the house. He followed Bertie up the stairs to Elizabeth's bedroom. The women all traipsed behind him like a trail of grim mourners, until Nana Rose came to her senses and started shouting orders to the entire household.

"Heat some water. Bring me a thin sharp knife. Build a fire in her room. Rags! We'll want plenty of rags. Needles. Catgut. Find some brandy or port. There must be some alcohol around here somewhere. And salve. Lavinnia, get the laudanum. Blythe, I'll need your steady hands."

Trace laid Lizzy on clean white sheets. A dark red stain fanned out under her shoulder. "I'll go for a physician."

"Can't!" Bertie ordered as she hurriedly built a fire. "The sawbones won't keep mum."

"Shooting our Lizzy wasn't enough?" Nana Rose nudged Trace out of the way. "You wish to see her hanged as well?" The old woman carefully untied the makeshift breastplate and removed it.

Bertie stared at Trace, troubled. "Best to come

straight out and tell us what's in the cards. Not much sense patching her up for the gallows. Too much grief, that way."

He turned away from Bertie's question, back to the woman he had loved. Lizzy lay dying, a thin chemise barely concealing her breasts. *Pale enticing flesh. Red alarming blood. Sweet sinful black tresses. Pure white linen.* His jaw tightened so fiercely his head hurt. *Black or white?*

If he didn't wake up from this nightmare, madness would take him. He raked a hand into his hair, trying to hold onto his reeling mind. Suddenly, the air seemed to grow thin in the room. He forced himself to breathe, to cling to the things that kept his world tilted upright.

The fire began to crackle. Nana Rose put the knife into the flame. Bertie awaited his answer.

He took one last look at Elizabeth Claegburn before he spoke. "For all your sakes, I will not report any of this. But, neither can I traffic in lies. Lord Mulvern is a good man. The only father I've ever known. I cannot stay in the vicinity and fail to tell him the truth. I'll take my leave on the morrow. Your secret will be safe."

Bertie nodded. Nana Rose's shoulders sagged with relief.

"Now, we must get on with this." His voice sounded hollow, like someone giving orders from far away. "I'll hold her down while you clean and cauterize the wound."

"Won't do." Rose shook her head, more compassion in her voice than Trace had ever heard in it before. "Have to remove her clothes. Best be on your way. We know what to do."

"For pity's sake, you can't stand on decorum. I'm not leaving until I know she's in the clear. You'll need help holding her. Believe me, I've seen this procedure often enough on the battlefield."

Bertie moved protectively in front of the bed. "Not done to a woman you haven't."

Nana thrust her fists on her hips. "Not to my granddaughter."

Blythe floated into the room like a benign ghost, carrying salve and needle and thread. "No point arguing with Nana. Mind of granite."

"Exactly." The old woman came at Trace like a cantankerous goat, head down, ready to butt or shove him out of the room. "The sooner you leave, the sooner we can tend her wound." She grabbed hold of his arm and pushed him toward the door.

He stood firm. "This is nonsense. I've known her since we were in leading strings."

"A shame you didn't know her well enough not to shoot her." Rose glared at him. "And unless you want her to bleed to death, I suggest you find your way out the door." She pointed emphatically.

He shook his head. *Stubborn old woman.* "Who here has the strength to hold her down? Neither of you. She will fight, believe me. Which of you has the nerve to dig in her flesh and find the ball?"

Blythe, unblinking, completely calm, looked up at him. "I will remove the bullet."

Bertie clapped him on the shoulder. "Bonnie and I can hold her down. Tie her, if we have to. Don't worry, lad. We'll manage."

Bertie maneuvered him to the doorway, just as Bonnie rushed into the room holding a bottle aloft. "Found some brandy! Mother's coming with the laudanum."

He hesitated in the doorway beside Bertie. "You're certain you can manage? I don't like it."

"Quite certain," Bertie assured him.

"One request. If she should . . ." He couldn't bring himself to say it.

"Die?" Nana Rose frowned impatiently at him. "Hurry up. Leave, and she won't."

"If you would send word to me through my father. I—"

"Of course." Bertie nodded gravely.

He hurried out of the room, so that the women might get on with their task. From the bottom of the stairs, he heard Lizzy moaning. As he reached the front door, she cried out in such anguish he had to hold onto the doorframe. It was all he could do not to turn around and run back up those stairs. Naked or not, she needed him.

Oh, yes. She needed the man who shot her. Trace had not cried since his mother died. The turmoil in his heart threatened to undo him. Lavinnia walked up behind him and quietly rested her hand on his bowed shoulder. "All will be well. You'll see."

But, it would not. *Nothing would ever be right again.* Lizzy screamed. Her agony ripped him wide open. Trace stumbled out into the darkness to find his horse, tears washing down his cheeks.

Chapter 7

At midday, Trace set out in his stepfather's coach to journey to his mother's family estates in Northampton. He had intended to sleep longer, but his feather bed offered little respite from the discomfort of his mind. So, he packed up and said his good-byes. He stared out of the window at Claegburn Woods. *This time, he would not come back.*

The day was bright and fair, a perfect day for an imperfect purpose. He cursed the blasted sunshine, wishing instead for billowing clouds, wild winds, and a thrashing rain. In answer, birds twittered inanely.

The coach bumped unexpectedly and lurched to the side, skidding to a halt. A smooth road. Nothing there to break an axle on. He'd ridden down this road ten dozen times in the past weeks. What could be amiss? He peered out of the window and then closed his eyes tight, falling back against his seat, astonished. He must be dreaming, still in his bed, and this simply another fitful nightmare. But, no.

He flung the door open and charged out of the coach ready to strangle them—one and all. "This is outside of enough! Are you mad? It's broad daylight! You're bound to be seen. And who's taking care of Elizabeth?"

Bertie stood unmoved, black eye mask, absurd beard, a cocked French cap, and a rather capable looking over-and-under pointed directly at him. "Stand and deliver."

"Deliver what? Have your wits gone begging? I have no jewels. If you wanted blunt, I would gladly have obliged you without this charade."

"Quiet." She growled, and then gestured with her pistol. "Turn around. Do as I say. I'm not above putting a vent in your spleen."

"Have at it." He opened his arms wide. "I don't give a fig if you do."

From the rear of the coach, he heard a familiar old voice rasp. "Stop yammering with him and get on with it. Can't stand here all day. I've got mending to attend to." Trace turned to find Rose, in black pantaloons, a purple satin sash with eyeholes tied around her head, her hair waving wildly like a white bush, as she bound the footman's hands.

Trace shook his head in disbelief. "Heavens above, Bertie. What did you do? Bring them all?"

Lavinnia, scarcely disguised in a pirate's bandanna and mask, toddled toward him. "I don't usually come. Thought I'd better this time, what with Lizzy . . . Oh, but that's the point, isn't it?" She waggled her foil in his direction. "Come along without a fuss."

He heard light footfalls on the top of the coach. That, he suspected, must be one of the twins. In black men's garb, a small figure leapt nimbly down from the box. Bonnie.

Bertie hissed to the girl under her breath. "Did you pay them?"

"Oui!" Bonnie grinned, beneath a crooked beard. "I thought we agreed to tie this one up as well?"

"Mad as hatters, all of you. Reasonable human beings do not behave in this manner. Women, most of all. You're supposed to be the gentler sex—"

Nana Rose grumbled. "Get on with it. Don't feel like standing here all day listening to him prose on."

"Turn around." Bertie prodded Trace's shoulder.

What ought I do? What can I do, aside from thrashing the lot of them—widows, spinsters, and chits? Hardly the gentlemanly thing. He shook his head and turned around.

Lavinnia nudged him in the side with her foil, obviously unaware of the sharpness of the point. "Bend down. It's this wretched head-sack. I can't reach. Now there's a good lad."

A good lad. Lunatics. Am I nine? And this a parlor game? They bound his hands securely and shrouded his head in one of the highwayman's infamous black hoods.

It was a dark bumpy trip in the back of their old dogcart. He hadn't the least notion why they bothered to hide his eyes. From the turns and condition of the roads, he knew exactly where they were taking him. What he could not comprehend was their purpose.

"Do you think I don't know where we are?" When they arrived at the Dower House, they led him upstairs. "Did she die? Is that it? This is retribution? If so, I welcome it. Do your worst. I deserve to be punished for not seeing what was directly under my nose. I failed her. Failed my stepfather. Chased a phantom that didn't exist."

The Dower House thieves were oddly silent. They locked him in a closet. Bound and blind. What were they planning? Leave him here to rot. He could, without a doubt, wrestle his hands free of the ropes and kick the door down. Instead, he sagged against the wall. What did it matter? If, indeed, Lizzy had died, he may as well follow suit. Weariness settled into his soul. He closed his eyes, hoping sleep would take him, but, like his fitful struggle the previous night, he found no pardon in the darkness.

Time amassed itself in indecipherable clumps. When they finally opened the door, he didn't know if it had been two days or two hours. Only his bladder marked the time, and it was full. "I need to relieve myself."

"In a moment," came the delicate reply. Blythe. Leading him gently by the hand, was she helping him escape? Or following orders from the madwomen of the Dower House?

"Where are you taking me?"

"To wash up and make ready." She loosened the hood and slid it up over his head.

The sudden rush of daylight blinded him more than the darkness had. "Make ready for what?"

Blythe untied his hands without answering. "You will find everything you need here. Your word, sir, that you won't climb out the window?"

He made no promise. He'd jolly well climb out of Bedlam if, and when, he pleased.

She shrugged and left him standing in the small

bedroom, in the welcome company of a chamber pot and a washstand.

Bertie scratched at the door before she burst in. "Excellent. You're up and about. No worse for the wear, I see."

She behaved as if nothing were amiss, as if he'd been taking a nap, and this merely a dream run amok. It was entirely possible that his coach had skidded sideways and crashed. He'd hit his head, and this was a convoluted delusion of his unconscious mind. He well remembered wounded soldiers, in their stupors, crying out at invisible dragons and fantastic monsters. A shame his infertile mind could only drum up a slew of mad old ladies.

Lavinnia ambled gaily into the room carrying a bundle, which she plopped on the bed. "Everything is ready. Let's see if these fit."

She held a long black gown up to his shoulders. "Oh dear, he's broader than I anticipated."

Bertie snorted. "It'll do. Only for one day, after all."

"What is it for?" Trace couldn't keep the snarl out of his voice. "Burial garb?"

"Oh, good heavens, no." Lavinnia twittered. Her faded gold ringlets bounced ridiculously under her mobcap. "Although, I suppose, if you think of it, in one fashion it may well signify a death."

"Enough jabbering. Put the robe on him." Bertie reached for a lump of wadding and shook it out. "Lord Mulvern will be here shortly."

"Mulvern! Blast it all, Bertie! What's my stepfather got to do with any of this? One thing to waylay me, but if you've harmed one hair on his—"

Bertie held up her hand. "Arriving on his own

accord. And I'll thank you to mind your tongue around gentlewomen, young man." She glanced pointedly at Lavinnia.

The widow smiled graciously at him and shook out the black cloak. "Oh, never mind that. Bound to be overwrought, isn't he?"

Overwrought? He laughed sourly. *Am I overwrought, or on the verge of joining ranks and becoming a bedlamite myself?* He allowed plump little Lavinnia to slide the garment on his arms, tug, and adjust it to fit his shoulders.

"That will suffice." Bertie prodded him forward. "Across the hall with you then."

They led him into the parlor.

"Lizzy!" *Alive. Thank God!* A part of his heart sprang back to life. At least, in all this madness, there was good news.

She sat in a peculiar enclosure, a square table turned on its side, boxing her in. Elizabeth lowered her head, averting her eyes from his, arm and shoulder bound in white bandages, her pallor ashen. *She should be in bed.*

The rest of the room had been oddly rearranged. Bertie guided him toward the far end, where a small desk sat, each of the legs propped up on a stack of books. The old Elizabethan chair Bertie was so fond of sat behind it raised up on an old woodbin.

"Sit." Bertie ordered.

He recognized the tableau then. Guessed their plan. Chairs arranged to mimic the assizes. Elizabeth sitting in a makeshift docks. "I'll have no part in this!"

Bertie folded her arms across her sagging bosom. "You will. Or do I have to get my blunderbuss?"

He stepped toward her. "You may choose whichever weapon from your arsenal you desire. I won't do it."

Lavinnia patted his arm, like he was a small boy she could cajole into behaving properly. "You won't do *what*, dear?"

"Judge. Judge her. I won't."

"Already have, I'd say." Bertie muttered, while fiddling with the wadding in the wig she held.

"She's right, you know." Earnestness sat oddly on Lavinnia's normally buoyant face. "The least you can do is finish the job."

Rose snarled at him from the doorway. "Unless you're a coward."

He held his roiling temper in check. "This is nonsense! If you insist on judgment, call a magistrate."

"Should arrive at any moment." Bertie held up the wig as if sizing it to his head.

He glared at her, too late remembering exactly who the magistrate was.

Lavinnia smiled at him. "Naturally, we all hold our magistrate in high esteem, but do you think your steppapa would be able to send the women of his own house to Newgate?"

"Humph. I say, he would do it in a trice." Nana Rose snapped her fingers.

Lavinnia shook her head mournfully. "No. It would break the dear man's heart. It falls to you, Trace. You are the only one who can judge fairly."

"Fairly? Judge her, fairly? Don't you know—"

"Yes. Are you daft? Of course, we know." Nana Rose marched toward him. "Lavinnia's idea to put you up to this. Knew you loved her. Saved the gel's life, didn't you? But you also had the backbone to turn your back on her because of her crimes."

"Do you see?" Lavinnia asked brightly, as if it were simple mathematics, the adding of two numbers to arrive at a sum.

He did not. This was some convoluted female logic designed to muddle a man's thinking. Eve, making Adam take a bite. They surrounded him, an army of females.

Bertie tried to elucidate. "A military man, you're the only one who wouldn't whitewash it. Go by the rules, don't you, lad?"

He frowned. They were trying to trick him. But, this line of reasoning tempted him too much not to refine upon it for this merry band of thieves. "Without laws, society would be intolerable. Ruthless. Anarchy. No one, *not even you, ladies,* would be safe."

"Exactly." Lavinnia nodded. "And yet, you didn't report our Lizzy."

His breath seemed to hang up in his neck somewhere. He glanced uncomfortably at the docks and caught Elizabeth peering attentively in his direction. She looked away.

He didn't know what to say.

"That's how we know you're the perfect man to act as judge. 'Justice tempered with mercy.' Mr. Milton said that." Lavinnia seemed quite pleased with herself.

"Shakespeare," Nana Rose corrected.

"Oh, no, I'm certain it's Milton."

"No matter." Rose waved away her daughter-in-law's protestations. "Point is, the gel won't eat." She nodded in Lizzy's direction. "Lost the will to live. Can't force her to get well, now can we? This is the only way."

"Yes. We've all agreed. After you hear our case, we'll abide by your decision, no matter what it is. We trust you'll choose the wisest course. If you think we should turn ourselves in, we will. They might hang us. But, I rather think, it would be deportation."

Bertie brightened. "Australia. Whales in that hemisphere. Wouldn't mind seeing another part of the world—"

"Bertie!" Nana Rose snapped.

"This would be a terrible burden to leave on your stepfather's shoulders." Lavinnia took the old parliamentary wig from Bertie and held it up to Trace. "Will you do it? For Lizzy's sake?"

Chapter 8

Trace took the bedraggled peruke Lavinnia offered and flopped it down on the writing desk. "No wig. If we're going to do this, we'll do it my way." He lifted the Elizabethan chair down from the makeshift dais and set it squarely on the floor. Frowning at the improvised docks imprisoning Lizzy, he started to move the inverted table away.

Lizzy put her hand on the edge. "Leave it."

"It's absurd."

"I prefer it."

He straightened and exhaled loudly. "As you wish."

A clatter in the foyer and a flurry of footsteps on the stairs alerted Trace to his stepfather's arrival.

Lord Mulvern charged into the parlor, breathless. "What's all this then? Note arrived. Said the highwaymen had been captured."

Lavinnia scurried to his side. "Yes. It's true. Come sit down." She led him to a chair on the right side of the room.

He continued to stand. Confusion registered on

his features as he absorbed the changes in the parlor and his stepson standing in the center. "Thought you took your leave this morning."

"As did I."

"Where is he then? The French rascal?"

Trace rubbed his jaw for a moment before answering. *No sense beating about the bush.* With a wry half-smile Trace waved his hand at the prisoner in the docks. "Allow me to introduce you to Lady Elizabeth Claegburn. Behold, my lord, the Frenchman." His gesture grandly encompassed the rest of the women standing mute in the parlor. "And her band of merry thieves."

He admired the way Lizzy unflinchingly met Lord Mulvern's astonished gaze.

Mulvern shook his head. "Called me here for a jest? A prank? Well, I am not amused. Ain't funny, lad." He frowned. "What happened to her arm?"

"I shot her." Trace waited for the truth to settle on his stepfather.

"Shot Lizzy? No. You wouldn't do such a thing, unless . . ." Mulvern dropped into the chair. "I don't believe it. No. Couldn't be. Not a woman."

While Mulvern sat muttering, digesting this unsettling revelation, Bertie rang a bell. "Oyez! Oyez! This hearing will now begin."

Trace frowned at her. "I think we can dispense with the formalities."

Bertie sniffed indignantly. "Court, lad. Calls for an air of authority."

He began to lose patience. "Do you realize, this is the only place in the civilized world where I am addressed as 'lad.' 'Captain,' I answer to. My father's family, in which I am the male heir, address me as 'Lord Ryerton.' If you wish to lend authority to these proceedings, try something other than 'lad.'"

"Very well, your Honor." Bertie smiled smugly. "Oyez! Court is now in session." She rang the bell.

Lord Mulvern glanced at his female relatives, his brow pinching into a thick gray V. "What's this? Court?"

Lavinnia stood beside him and patted his arm. "Yes. We rather hoped you would represent the Crown."

"Gad, must be a hallucination. A bad mushroom in my omelet."

Trace sat down facing them. "All too real, I'm afraid. They want to present their case to us."

Lavinnia cleared her throat. "For my first witness I will call the Dowager Countess of Mulvern, Lady Rose."

Rose sat grudgingly in the witness chair. Before anyone asked her a question, she pointed her finger at Lord Mulvern. "None of this would be happening if it weren't for you! Murderer. Ought to be you sitting in the docks, instead of our Lizzy."

Mulvern slapped his hands against his knees. "How many times are you going to dredge up that old saw?"

"Till somebody listens. Till it's you swinging from Tyburn. And now, on account of you, Lizzy might—"

"Told you a hundred times, I did not kill Royce. The mere suggestion is—"

Rose thumped her fist on the chair arm. "He died directly after you went to his room."

"Of lung fever, Rose. That's why I came. To see my brother before he—"

"No. You hated him. You were always jealous. You wanted the title. And then my sons . . . You couldn't wait to turn us out of Claegburn."

"You go too far, old woman. You know full well, I

offered you, *all of you,* a place in the manor. Deuced nervous about it, too, what with you running about calling me a murderer at every turn. Half thought you'd poison m'food.

"Considered it," Rose muttered venomously under her breath.

Mulvern ignored her. "But, no. You wouldn't have any of it. And now this! If you wanted funds, you should have applied to me."

"What? Come begging to *you?*"

This tirade was going nowhere. Trace decided to put an end to it, but Lizzy beat him to it.

"Stop!" She half stood in the box, but then sagged back into her chair. "Stop. You can't blame him any longer. And above all, not for this."

Nana Rose crossed her arms defensively, but said nothing.

Lizzy rested her head on her hand. "It's so much easier to have a name, a face, to turn our anger at, Nana. Pneumonia took grandfather. And I knew my parent's carriage wheel broke of its own accord." She glanced at the women of her family. "So grotesquely unfair that they should be crushed, killed in that accident, and I thrown free." She shook her head. "In lieu of hating providence, it was easier to blame Lord Mulvern." She glanced at her uncle, sorrowful. "I'm sorry. This is none of your doing. This is owing to our own foolish pride."

Nana Rose stood up. "What of the tenants! That's his doing. Without us, what would've happened to the Turners, or Bernards, or . . . ? Well, you know how many of them we helped. It's all in the book. He should have been taking care of them and the estates. Shameful how he let it run to shambles."

Lavinnia clapped her hands together, signaling

a close to the discussion. "Thank you very much, Rose. Step down, please. Bonnie, dear, will you come to testify?"

Trace held up his hand, forestalling them. "What book?"

Lavinnia smiled graciously. "The accounting book, of course, your Lordship."

He glanced wildly at Lizzy. "You kept a record?"

She raised a small accounting book from her lap just high enough for him to see the deuced thing really existed.

Bonnie trudged up and took her grandmother's place in the witness chair. She appealed to Trace straight off. "You can't blame Lizzy alone. She wanted to take Blythe and me to London for a proper season, so we wouldn't end up old maids like her and Bertie."

The chit didn't mince words. She may as well have plunged a knife into Trace's heart.

Old maid. Lizzy thought she was an old maid. He'd left her here alone, uncertain of her expectations. He'd ridden off to the battlefield thinking their future was obvious, a certainty. She'd concluded it was a lost dream.

He pressed his lips together and lowered his head to his hands. What a mess they'd all made of things. He stood up, suddenly, and went to the prisoner's box. If only she'd look at him. He shrugged out of the black robe and tossed it aside. She still would not meet his gaze.

Even bruised and pale, her face was beautiful to him—not necessarily the lines or features, but the woman that face described. He knew then, he would have come back for her. He was a fool to have thought otherwise. She meant everything to him. He would ride into Hades if he had to. He held out his hand. "I would like to see that book, if I may?"

Lizzy handed it to him, reluctantly, like a student handing in an examination book, knowing full well the answers therein would add up to a failing grade.

He tried to relieve her trepidation. "Four years. How many coaches could you have robbed? Only a handful, surely."

By her raised brow, Trace knew he'd been optimistic. He glanced at the other women, all carefully avoiding his inspection. He returned to the dubious comfort of Bertie's chair.

"Not much else to do in this part of the empire," Bertie muttered.

Bonnie sat watching, fidgeting nervously, as he turned the pages. His heart sank lower with every carefully written ledger sheet.

Lavinnia cleared her throat. "Please bear in mind, your Honor. We are all guilty."

"Yes, it's on all of us," Bonnie added.

"Don't listen to them," Lizzy urged, at last speaking. "It was my doing. They never would've fallen into it, if I hadn't . . ."

He didn't look up. He kept his eyes on the page. If he looked up now, she would know how intensely he admired her courage, how this whole thing was breaking him inside. She'd done it for them, yet she willingly took full responsibility. He tightened his jaw painfully to keep his emotions in check, and kept reading and tallying.

Lord Mulvern shook his head. "How bad is it, son?"

He couldn't answer yet, more pages to calculate.

When at last Trace closed the book, he stared thoughtfully at the ladies of the Dower House. "You all agree to abide by my decision?"

They nodded, with varying degrees of reluctance.

"And, Lord Mulvern, do you agree as well?"

His stepfather rubbed at his temple, as if trying to find relief from a burgeoning megrim. "Whole thing is a confounded muddle. A scandalous tangle. Women of my own house—thieves? I can't comprehend it. And you, Lavinnia?" He cast a forlorn glance at the solicitor for the defense. "I was on the point of asking you to be my . . . had hoped you might consider . . ."

Lavinnia chewed the corner of her lip, but wisely didn't interrupt.

Lord Mulvern waved his hand, as if too weary to finish speaking his mind. "Yes. If you can sort it, Trace, then by all means, I'll stand with you."

Trace nodded. "And Lizzy? Will you submit to whatsoever punishment for your crimes I deem necessary?"

He thought it impossible that her face could turn any paler, but it did. *He must hurry.* She nodded, almost imperceptibly.

"Very well. I'm ready to state my verdict." *Ring the bell,* Trace thought. But Bertie the bell ringer gripped the edge of her seat, as frozen as the rest of them.

"Lady Elizabeth Claegburn, I find you guilty of armed robbery against the King's subjects."

She sagged.

He wanted to gather her up in his arms and hold her, but this was a moment she must bear on her own. A moment that would alter the course of their lives. "For these crimes, which are numerous," he held up the accounting book, "I order you to anonymously repay all that you have stolen."

Nana Rose jumped to her feet. "She can't! Look at her. How in heaven's name do you expect her to pay it back? It's spent. Tenants' roofs. Clothing. Food—"

Blythe stood up. "Our London fund. Take the London fund."

"Not nearly enough." Nana Rose planted her fists on her hips. "Impossible!"

"Silence." Trace held up his hand. "Sit down! You asked for judgment. I'm judging."

He turned back to Elizabeth. "However, I offer you an alternative sentence."

"Deportation?" Bertie asked.

He held up a silencing finger, before returning to his pale prisoner. "I will pay your debt."

"No." Lizzy looked up at him, startled. "I couldn't. It's not your debt. You shouldn't have to pay for my—"

"No, lad. She's right. Not your debt." Lord Mulvern protested. "They gave the money to my tenants. Rose has the right of it. Should've fallen to me, anyway."

"A portion, perhaps. However, you, Lord Mulvern, will be held responsible for attending to their future with far more diligence. We will discuss that at length later. At the moment, Lady Elizabeth *must* answer her sentence."

Trace focused on Lizzy. "As your husband, your debt would become mine. I will pay it off immediately."

"As my . . . ?"

"Yes. I'm offering a lifetime sentence, not as a criminal, but as my wife. During which time, I believe you are legally bound to love, honor, cajole, play chess, kiss, raise children, and did I mention love?" He was certain he had.

Lizzy swallowed hard. Her eyes shimmered with impending tears. Trace feared what he saw there: remorse, shame, and reticence. *She was going to refuse him.* He shook his head. "Oh, Lizzy, don't say no. I beg you. I'm going to pay it off anyway, and gladly. But say you'll have me? Say it!"

She covered her mouth with her fingers, hiding her quivering lips. He waited for her answer. It seemed like an eternity before she managed a choked reply. "But you said you couldn't love a thief."

He felt a tug of hope. "Evidently, I was wrong."

She smiled then, and nodded, radiant as an angel under a waterfall of tears.

Good thing he knew what that nod meant. He yanked away the annoying prisoner's box and scooped her up into his arms. "Yes," she whispered into his neck. "Yes."

He kissed her, his sweet Lizzy, to the accompaniment of elder women sighing, and younger women oh-ing.

"And now, my love, it's time you rested." He carried her away from the courtroom and off to her bedroom.

He laid her down on the bed, the dark stain of blood from the previous night gone and fresh white linen in its place. He sat down beside her, smoothing strands of midnight black hair back from her wet cheeks. Her color looked better already.

He could not resist kissing her once more. "No more tears, Lizzy, my sweet. Rest. Gather your strength. You have a long and tedious sentence ahead of you. A lifetime of loving me will not be easy. Years and years of kisses, and—" He grinned at her speculatively.

She laughed, and with her good arm pulled him down to her eager mouth.

He smiled into her greedy kiss. *Perhaps not so tedious after all.*

The Rebel and the Rogue

Mona Gedney

Chapter 1

Vivian Woodruff moved back a step, for the man next to her was standing far too close. His nearness, in fact, made her long for a sharply pronged fork or perhaps her sewing scissors, so that she could hint at her displeasure. She did not even like being in the same room with Paul Lanyon, and she most certainly had no wish to be the object of his attentions. Least of all did she wish to be backed into a corner from which he showed no sign of allowing her to escape. A potted palm occupied most of the corner, and it showed no sign of moving over to allow her more space. Mr. Lanyon's appearance was considered elegant, she knew, but his manner was—in her view, at least—repellent.

"Come now, Vivian," he murmured, employing all of what he obviously thought his irresistible charm as he bent still closer to her, his hand on her arm. She shivered involuntarily at his touch and he smiled, misreading her reaction.

"Come and dance with me," he urged, his voice

low and intimate. "Allow me to have the honor of breaking the hearts of all the young men in the room."

Miss Woodruff was unmoved by his use of hyperbole. She glanced pointedly about the room, which did not appear to be teeming with young men eager to throw themselves at her feet.

"Yes, I do see them lined up, all of them aching to stand up with me," she replied dryly. "I daresay they could not decide who is to have the honor first and have stepped into the card room to cast lots to decide the matter."

She did not add that if she had seen an available gentleman, she would have snapped him up in an instant and made her escape. She had even eyed one elderly gentleman who had tottered by on a cane, but he had managed to reach the safety of the card room before she could make up her mind whether to push Mr. Lanyon aside and whisk him, cane and all, onto the dance floor. The elderly gentleman would now be safely ensconced in a chair, playing whist with his companions, she thought sadly, while she was left to fend off an unwanted suitor.

Mr. Lanyon looked taken aback by both her retort and her tone, and he attempted a more straightforward appeal. "But, Vivian, be reasonable, dear girl. You cannot wish to stand here while everyone else is dancing."

"On the contrary, Mr. Lanyon," she replied crossly, drawing as far away from him as the limited space would allow and pressing dangerously close to the potted palm. Soon, she thought bitterly, she would be forced to climb up into the pot and try to retreat behind the plant. "I really have no desire to dance just now. Nor am I your 'dear girl.' I *do* wish, sir, that you would address me as Miss Woodruff."

"Nonsense, Vivian!" he protested, his eyes regarding her with foxlike intensity. "We need not stand on ceremony, you and I. We are very nearly family, you know."

She looked at him with open distaste. Her stepmother had told her that many women regarded him as a particularly fine-looking gentleman, but she was not among their number. His pale eyes were set too close together, his chin was weak, and she had the distinct impression that beneath his polished manners and appearance lurked a most unpleasant individual.

"If we are truly all family, sir, I wonder that you appear interested in establishing what could only be considered a most unhealthy and ill-considered relationship," she responded frankly, not smiling in return. "In fact, Mr. Lanyon, there are moral and legal laws that prohibit that sort of thing."

"You are always so very *quick*, are you not?" He laughed uncomfortably, still trying to maintain the fiction that they were exchanging a light volley of pleasantries. Her manner was not at all what he expected of a young lady new to London and the *ton*. By rights, she should be impressed by his gallantry and attentiveness, not acting as though she had just stepped upon a snake on the garden path. He glanced about helplessly for a moment, apparently trying to think of a way to regroup before trying to press his advantage once more.

"Well, if you will not dance, at least allow me to bring you some refreshment, my dear," he added, doubtless feeling that a slight respite from her company would be welcome.

Vivian brightened. She, too, welcomed anything that would cause him to be absent for at least a few minutes, allowing her some breathing space and the opportunity to remove herself from this corner, where he could entrap her so easily. Another thought suddenly occurred to her. Having something in her hand could be very useful if Mr. Lanyon continued his unwelcome attentions. If she could not have her sewing scissors, she might at least have something. She had even thought of swinging her reticule at him, but it was too small and silken to have any effect.

While he was gone, she looked about her for an ally, but she could see no one except her stepmother, who was standing with her back to Vivian. Lady Farrington, she knew, would be no help at all, because she was clearly encouraging Mr. Lanyon's attentions.

Since Vivian had arrived in London only a fortnight ago from Mrs. Chester's Seminary for Young Ladies, she knew very few people here apart from her family. She would have given much just then to have seen Louisa Thurston's cheerful face among the throng. She sighed and put that thought away, for she feared it was most unlikely that she would see her good friend again. Becoming a watering pot over the loss of Louisa would do neither of them any good just now. She reminded herself firmly that she must keep her attention upon solving the problem at hand, for Mr. Lanyon would soon return, and she had no one to rely upon except herself.

She had not been long at the ball, but he had descended upon her almost immediately. Lady Farrington had removed herself from their vicinity with an alacrity that made Vivian certain that the meeting had been agreed upon beforehand. A pleasant-faced young man had started toward them once, very likely intending to ask her to stand up with him, but Mr. Lanyon had managed to frown him away. She looked about for the young man now, hoping that he might take advantage of Lanyon's absence. She would be delighted if her nemesis returned to find her already on the dance floor, safely beyond his reach.

To her disappointment, she saw that the young man was already dancing, and an earnest survey of the room failed to reveal anyone else who might help her. In a distant corner, however, she caught a glimpse of a very tall, very dark gentleman who looked vaguely familiar to her. She watched him for a moment, and suddenly she realized who he was, for she had seen a miniature with his likeness. He was, she was certain, Anthony Mallory! Once the initial shock of this realization had passed, she scrutinized him carefully. Because of Louisa, he had been a subject of considerable interest to her for several months, and she took advantage of this opportunity to study him closely.

She must have been staring more intently than she realized, for Mallory suddenly looked up from his conversation with another gentleman, frowning slightly, as though aware that someone was watching him. Vivian turned her eyes hastily, but not in time. He had seen her looking at him, and he bowed in her direction, looking amused.

Feeling more like a schoolgirl than ever, Vivian regarded the toes of her green silk slippers with rather more interest than they merited until Lanyon appeared again. If she had been able to think of a place to remove herself to, she would have done so, but the card room, she knew, offered no escape and retiring to the darkness of the garden would convey entirely the wrong message to Mr. Lanyon. Whether she wished it or not, for the moment, she was trapped once more, but she was careful to position herself away from the potted palm and the corner.

"Here, Vivian," he said, again lowering his voice and investing even this innocent remark with an air of suggestive intimacy, "a glass of ratafia should restore your spirits." His voice, she thought in disgust, was almost oily.

"Thank you, Mr. Lanyon," she replied, placing the emphasis upon *mister* so that he would not mistake their relationship. "My spirits do not require restoration, however, and I do not care for ratafia— but the glass of claret will suit me very well."

He had no opportunity to remonstrate, for she had taken the glass of claret firmly in hand before he realized what she intended to do.

He leaned toward her, smiling still, although the pleasant expression was clearly forced, and he reached for the glass.

"I will just take that, Vivian. A young girl has no need of—"

He had no opportunity to inform her what she had no need of, however, for a deep, lazy voice suddenly commanded their attention.

"How very unchivalrous of you, Lanyon. I was just thinking that the young lady might enjoy a glass of champagne rather than claret, but I see that you are planning to give her no choice at all. Indeed, you appear to be commandeering her drink for yourself. I am quite shocked at such unmannerly behavior."

The speaker's expression and his tone both indicated that he was anything but shocked, for his eyes were bright with amusement as he watched Lanyon's mouth open and close convulsively. Quite like a fish jerked from its safe, stagnant waters, Vivian thought, watching his discomfiture with pleasure. He was clearly unhappy at the unexpected appearance of Anthony Mallory.

"Please allow me to bring you a glass of champagne, miss," Mallory said, bowing to Vivian.

"You are very kind, sir, but that is not necessary," she said, dropping a curtsy to Mallory and smiling up at him. She had not realized how very tall a man he was, for he towered over both of them, even as he made his bow.

"Then perhaps you would do me the honor of dancing with me, Miss—" He paused a moment as though searching his memory.

"Woodruff, sir," she replied. "Miss Vivian Woodruff. And I would be delighted to dance with you."

"I cannot allow you to do so, Vivian," said Lanyon, attempting to gather the tatters of his dignity. "Mr. Mallory is scarcely a suitable partner for you."

Before Mallory could respond, Vivian had wheeled upon him. "How *dare* you tell me what I may and may not do, sir!" she replied, her dark eyes snapping. "You take far too much upon yourself!"

"You know nothing of the matter," said Lanyon firmly, attempting to hold himself taller, uncomfortably aware as he did so that Mallory still stood several inches above him. "Your mother would not wish it, Vivian."

Her face was still bright with anger, but her reply was icy. "My mother is long dead, Mr. Lanyon, and I cannot think you are privy to her wishes."

She turned toward Anthony Mallory, clearly about to walk away with him, and Mr. Lanyon made the unfortunate error of catching her by the arm.

"You know that I am referring to Lady Farrington, Vivian. I must insist that—"

Infuriated by this further attempt to restrain her physically, Vivian turned upon him in a flash and flung her glass of claret into his face. Red wine soaked his immaculate cravat and his white waist-coat and dripped from his pale face and brown hair. A shocked silence fell over their corner of the room as several of the other guests turned to stare.

Mallory quickly interrupted the tableau, how-ever. He took the glass from Vivian's hand and set it carefully on a nearby table, then offered her his arm and cheerfully advised the paralyzed victim about the care of his wardrobe. He removed a white handkerchief from his pocket and handed it to Lanyon, who accepted it as though he were in a trance.

"Red wine is the very devil for staining, Lanyon. Best get yourself home quickly so that your man can take care of that for you."

And with the briefest of nods, he led Vivian toward the dance floor.

"I can see, Miss Woodruff, that it is best not to make you angry," he remarked lightly. "I shall take great care not to do so."

Vivian's cheeks were scarlet. "You must think me shamefully ill-bred," she responded. "I do not normally behave so poorly."

"I should imagine that you are not normally of-fered such provocation." He studied her for a mo-ment. "Lanyon appeared to be taking a great deal for granted in his treatment of you."

"Yes, he was, indeed," Vivian replied grimly, "but I daresay he will think carefully before he does so again."

A brief smile glittered on Mallory's dark face. "I am certain that he will. I have seldom seen anyone look so thunderstruck. One does not expect to be suddenly set upon by a kitten."

Vivian stopped abruptly. "I am *not* a kitten, Mr. Mallory! You would be sadly mistaken to think so!"

"No, no," he hastened to assure her. "Pray believe me, miss, that I saw the error of Lanyon's judgment even before the claret went flying. I am merely commenting upon what *he* must have been thinking."

She relaxed and allowed herself a brief smile at the memory of Mr. Lanyon's expression of disbelief. That alone—to say nothing of the relief of ridding herself, at least temporarily, of his company—would have been enough to make the evening a success in her eyes. She had carefully avoided looking about her to see the reactions of others, particularly that of her stepmother, to her treatment of Mr. Lanyon. She had no doubt that she would be the subject of countless critical discussions, but the thought did not trouble her.

"I do not believe he expected it," she conceded modestly to Mr. Mallory, "but then neither did I. It simply happened."

"And I am certain that Mr. Lanyon will be much more circumspect in his treatment of you in the future because of it," Mr. Mallory assured her, leading her into the dance.

Vivian was less certain of this, but she nodded, trying to blot out the thoughts that were suddenly crowding out all her pleasure in routing Mr. Lanyon. She knew that there would be repercussions from her actions when she returned home that evening, and she had no doubt that they would be unpleasant.

She had grown weary of the reproofs of her very

critical stepmother, but she had no way to escape them. Lady Farrington seemed never to tire of finding fault with Vivian—with her appearance, her manner, her conversation. Upon the death of Vivian's father several years earlier, her stepmother had inherited a very comfortable fortune. Vivian, however, had inherited the bulk of the estate, which would become hers when she married.

Her stepmother had recently remarried, acquiring Lord Farrington with little problem, for she was still a lovely woman—and now a woman of substantial means. Vivian, having no other family, had remained with her stepmother after her father's death, although most of her time had been spent at boarding school or at the home of her best friend, Louisa Thurston.

Now, however, she was to make her home in London with Lord and Lady Farrington. Although she had been with them only a fortnight, the two of them had appeared to dedicate themselves to making her life miserable, finding fault with her open manners and her habit of speaking her mind clearly on all subjects, whether invited to do so or not. She was determined to have the upper hand in her own affairs, and her stepparents had been spending their time trying to curb what they called her rebellious behavior.

However, despite his disapproval of her manners, Lord Farrington apparently had kept in mind the handsome fortune that Vivian would inherit upon her marriage. Therefore, since her arrival in London, he had sought to interest her in his youngest brother, the only one still unmarried. Vivian understood the purpose of Lord Farrington's thinly veiled attempts to thrust them together, and she was appalled by the thought of spending a single evening with Paul Lanyon—let alone a lifetime in his company. Nonetheless, she had begun to suspect that her stepparents were determined to keep her from forming any attachments so that Lanyon could fix his interests with her.

She sighed. She knew that she had not seen the last of Paul Lanyon by any means, and she had not yet developed a plan for handling the situation.

"Well, I admit that not every young woman finds me charming," said Mallory, smiling down at her ruefully, "but they do not usually give way to gusty sighs in the midst of a dance."

Despite her unhappy preoccupation, Vivian laughed. "Forgive me, Mr. Mallory. I was not sighing because of your company, I assure you. My mind had wandered to unhappy topics."

He nodded gravely, but his eyes were merry. "You relieve me," he returned. "I would scarcely be able to hold up my head if it were widely known that I had bored my dancing partner into a series of sighs and sad looks."

"I promise you that there will be no more sighing, sir."

She smiled up at him, wondering that such a large man could dance so gracefully. By great good fortune, they had missed the cotillion and stood up instead for the new dance that had taken England by storm—the beguiling waltz.

"I am quite afraid to look about me for fear of catching the eye of some disapproving lady," she confessed to him. "I know that my behavior will be thought scandalous, and that my stepmother will be horrified. I don't particularly mind for myself, but I know I shall be reprimanded."

"I must confess something to you, Miss Woodruff," he told her gravely. The merriment had faded from his eyes, and he appeared to be speaking seriously.

"And what might that be, Mr. Mallory?" she asked, determined to be cheerful, come what may.

"I am afraid that I am, at this very moment, the cause of your scandalous behavior."

"What do you mean?" she asked, puzzled by his cryptic remark. Insofar as she could see, flinging the glass of claret had been the scandal.

"You are dancing with a ne'er-do-well, of course," he informed her. "Mr. Lanyon told you as much— but that would not be enough by itself to create a scandal. The real problem is that we are dancing the waltz together."

He was angry with himself for not having thought of this beforehand, and then he was surprised by the fact that it mattered to him at all. Why should he be bothered by creating a possible problem for a young girl he scarcely knew? He never troubled himself with matters of reputation.

"Yes, I know," Vivian replied, still puzzled. "It is a lovely dance. We learned it at school when it became all the rage."

"It seems that there are rules that regulate the behavior of young ladies very closely, Miss Woodruff," he explained to her. "If we were at Almack's, for instance, you would not be allowed to dance the waltz unless you had received the permission of the patronesses."

"Indeed?" she responded. "Then it is fortunate that we are not at Almack's, is it not?" It appeared to her that he was making a great piece of work about nothing.

"I am afraid that it is probably worse that we are not," he told her. "There, at least, your behavior would be carefully governed, and once you had received permission, you might dance the waltz everywhere without fear of reproach. Now, however, you are a young lady newly come to town, not yet secure in your reputation."

He looked down at her without smiling, for, indeed, he had not thought about this aspect of rescuing her from her tormentor until it was already too late. He had simply noticed a pretty young girl who had been watching him, and had then been annoyed by Lanyon's boorish behavior. He had not thought beyond that moment.

"Have you already received your voucher for Almack's, Miss Woodruff?" he asked.

She shook her head. Her stepmother had requested a voucher for her, but she had not yet been invited to appear at Almack's. It really did not particularly matter to her, but Lady Farrington had been quite obsessed by the need for Vivian to receive a voucher. No doubt she planned for Vivian to spend her time there in the company of Mr. Lanyon.

"Then I am afraid that by waltzing with me here, before your invitation to that Inner Sanctum, you may have unwittingly done yourself damage," he said. "Lady Jersey is here tonight, and if she has seen you, she might well hold this waltz against you. They can be ridiculously strict about what they consider proper behavior." He did not add that it was particularly ridiculous when the reputations of the patronesses, that of Lady Jersey included, were scarcely spotless.

Mallory halted abruptly and led her from the floor, glancing about as he did so. "I don't see her just now, but that does not mean she might not learn about our dance. I will see what I can do to mend matters with her if she does, indeed, hear that a young woman has been waltzing in public before her admittance to Almack's."

He did not add, Vivian noted gratefully, the matter of the glass of claret. That alone would be quite enough to make her *persona non grata* with the patronesses of Almack's. It seemed to her quite noble that he was taking the blame upon himself.

"They call Lady Jersey 'Silence,'" he told her in a low voice, sounding amused once again, "because she never ceases talking. So I daresay that I can work my way around her if she believes you were being imposed upon and that I was at fault— because I generally am, you know. She will be delighted to have the opportunity to abuse me to my face for all the sins, real and imaginary, that she believes I may have committed. It will put her in a splendid mood, and she will undoubtedly send you a voucher."

"How very kind you are, Mr. Mallory," she said gratefully. At least she might be spared Lady Farrington's recriminations for throwing away her chances at Almack's. Although Vivian did not really care, she did grow weary of being constantly scolded.

Mr. Mallory looked down at her with a very odd expression.

"Now that is a word seldom used to describe me, Miss Woodruff," he replied. "I shall have to consider how I feel about it."

That was the end of their conversation, however, for Lady Farrington appeared just then, casting a disapproving look at Mr. Mallory and summoning Vivian to her side.

"Are we leaving already?" Vivian asked.

"Thanks to your outrageous behavior, we most certainly are," Lady Farrington assured her in an agitated whisper. "David has sent for our carriage, and poor Paul has already left. I have never been so mortified in my life!"

Chapter 2

The confrontation at home was all that Vivian had expected it to be. She seated herself comfortably in the drawing room, for she knew that her stepmother's recriminations would not be brief.

"Really, Vivian! You simply *must* remember what you owe to your position!"

The lovely Lady Farrington eyed her stepdaughter with extreme irritation, remembering, however, not to allow that irritation to cause her to wrinkle her flawless face. She was sharply aware that her complexion was not as youthful as it had once been, and she had no intention of creating wrinkles over an ungrateful stepchild.

"And just what *is* my position, Rebecca?" inquired the ingrate. "And precisely why must I uphold it?"

"Everyone knows that you are my stepdaughter," said Lady Farrington, attempting a display of patience that she was very far from feeling, "and David is everywhere known, a man greatly admired in

London. You *must* realize that your improper behavior reflects poorly upon both of us."

Vivian noticed that there was no mention of her having disgraced her own dead father—only her stepmother and her new husband. Her response was direct and merciless, for she believed absolutely that the best defense was a good offense.

"One would think that I had been dancing on tabletops—or that I had damped my muslin gown so that it clung to me like a second skin!" replied Vivian, watching with amusement as Lady Farrington flushed as she added the last observation.

She knew very well that Lady Farrington had created a scandal in her girlhood by doing just that. Not by dancing on the tabletops, perhaps, but certainly by damping her gown and leaving off her shift. Vivian pursued her advantage, certain that it would be only momentary.

"And just what have *I* done that is improper, Rebecca? Said something that I wanted to say instead of simpering like a fool? Kept Paul Lanyon from taking liberties with me that he had no right to take? My father reared me to have opinions of my own and to act on my own behalf."

"And just see where that has got us!" retorted her stepmother. "If you had been taught to keep a civil tongue and behave as a young girl should, you would not have flung your glass of wine in Paul's face tonight! Poor man, how very humiliating for him!"

Vivian was unmoved. Her stepmother had been finding fault with her ever since her father's death—something that she would never have dared to do while he was still alive. Vivian had become hardened to her comments, so much so that she paid no attention to them even when there was some truth in them.

"I shall do so again if he speaks to me in the same manner—or if he dares to lay hold of me and act as though he can order me about."

"Honestly, Vivian, can you not see the difference between a gentleman like Paul and a rogue like Anthony Mallory?" demanded Lady Farrington.

"I most certainly can. It is Mallory who is the gentleman and Lanyon who is the rogue," responded Vivian. "I have only to compare the way each one treats me to know that!"

"You heedless chit!" Her stepmother began to pace the floor angrily, forgetting to keep her face calm and unlined. "Paul told me that he warned you against Mallory, but that you ignored him! Bad enough to make a spectacle of yourself by throwing the wine on Paul, but then you must stand up with a man who is noted for leaving a path of destruction behind him! Why, he has ruined more lives than you could ever imagine!"

"I don't believe it," said Vivian flatly. Actually, of course, she suspected there might be some truth in her stepmother's words, but she was determined not to agree with her. "I found him to be a charming companion! Far better than your dear Paul!"

"You have no notion what you are talking about!" replied Lady Farrington. "You should be deeply grateful that a gentleman like Paul Lanyon shows an interest in you!"

Vivian looked anything but grateful as she responded to her stepmother's call for gratitude.

"Mr. Lanyon appears to feel that he has the right to tell me what to do, but let me tell you two things very clearly, Rebecca. He has no right to order me about, and I most certainly shall never marry him, if that is what you and David have in mind!"

Her indignation about her treatment that evening had reappeared as though it were happening again, and she sprang to her feet as she spoke. The memory of Paul Lanyon's face, brought far too close to her own, still had the power to bring anger and distaste bubbling to the surface. It really did not matter to her that he was David's brother, or that she had made a spectacle of both of them by her reaction to his advances. She would do it again in an instant.

"You will do just as you are bade to do, my girl!" Lady Farrington replied sharply, abandoning all pretense of a reasonable approach. "You are still under our care, and so you shall remain! If your father had indulged you less, you would not be so wayward now!"

Turning, she swept from the room—or at least she would have if the hem of her gown had not caught upon the edge of a table, reducing her attempt at a grand exit to a hasty scramble as she caught a delicate china vase that almost tumbled to the floor.

Vivian allowed herself an indiscreet chuckle, and Lady Farrington glared at her, righted the vase, and flung herself from the room, closing the door behind her with great dignity, although it was clear that she wished to slam it so hard that everything in the room—including Vivian's teeth—would rattle.

Her unrepentant stepdaughter sank back onto her chair and sighed, all trace of amusement gone as she considered her situation. Lady Farrington would never tire of finding fault with her, of that she was certain. But what could she do about the problem? More to the point, what could she do about ridding herself of the loathsome Paul Lanyon?

Once she could have gone to Louisa Thurston and her mother for help, or at least stayed with them for a few weeks while she decided what course of action she could take, but now she did not even know where they were.

Of course, she thought slowly, it was possible she might be able to discover their whereabouts—now that she knew that Anthony Mallory was in London. He was not at all what she had expected; he had been surprisingly kind to her this evening.

Or he might be something quite different from what he appeared to be, she reminded herself. Her stepmother might well be right about him. There was no way at all to be certain. After all, she had only the sketchiest information about him— and all of it based on hearsay. Tonight was the only time that she had had the opportunity to observe him herself.

She knew that tomorrow night she would be attending yet another ball with her stepparents— and very likely with the loathsome Lanyon. If Mr. Mallory were also in attendance, perhaps she might take the opportunity to speak with him. And perhaps—just perhaps—he might be able to help her.

And, by the time the next evening had arrived, Vivian knew that she must have help.

Chapter 3

Lord and Lady Farrington took up their grievance with her at breakfast the morning after the ball. Neither of them usually appeared at that time. Lord Farrington preferred to go to his club, and his wife drank her chocolate in bed while she read her morning mail. Vivian had lived with them long enough to know that this change in their habits was not a good sign.

Lord Farrington cleared his throat importantly as a footman held his chair for him to be seated. He was a very slender, undistinguished man and, to atone for his lack of physical presence, he had long ago acquired the habit of clearing his throat and pausing portentously before making even the most trivial of comments. Today, however, he did have something of consequence to say.

"Vivian," he began finally, after waiting for a few moments and fixing her with a frosty stare.

"Yes, Lord Farrington?" she replied, determined to show that she was not at all intimidated by his manner. She had hoped to enjoy her tea and toast in peace, but she could see that was not to be.

"What you did last night," he continued in measured tones, "was completely unacceptable."

Then he paused and waited for her contrite response. Vivian merely took another bite of toast and reached for her teacup.

"Have you nothing to say to that, miss?" he asked, his voice rising slightly.

Vivian shook her head and calmly sipped her tea, looking for all the world as though he were discussing the roses in the garden.

"And why not?" he demanded, abandoning his stately manner. "Why do you not apologize for your outrageous behavior?"

"Because what Mr. Lanyon did was completely unacceptable." Vivian's voice was brisk and matter-of-fact. "Yet I know that you will say nothing at all to him about his behavior."

Lord Farrington did not flush when he grew angry. Instead, he seemed to grow even paler and his nose grew even more pinched.

"My brother did his best to keep you from dancing with a man who should not be accepted in polite society—and how did you repay him? I ask you that, miss? Describe what you had the brazen effrontery to do!"

"Your brother grabbed my arm and gave me an order, sir," she replied evenly, "and I threw the contents of my glass on him so that he would release me. He has no right to touch me or to command me."

"As a member of this family, he has every right—indeed, every duty to do so!" retorted Lord Farrington.

"I do not recognize such a right," replied Vivian,

her voice calm. "Indeed, I do not recognize him as a part of my family. Should he behave to me in such a manner again, he should expect precisely the same reaction."

At this, Lord Farrington appeared to gasp for air, and Vivian noted with interest that he and his brother were more alike than she had realized. They shared the same fishlike response to unwelcome surprises.

He turned to his wife when he finally managed to catch his breath.

"What do you mean to do about this, ma'am?" he demanded, neatly transferring the responsibility for the situation to Vivian's stepmother.

Lady Farrington shrugged. "I have told you that she has been too much indulged. Perhaps it would do her some good to be sent to Ardmore Hall."

Vivian knew that this was intended as a threat of punishment, that being banned to the country was what Lady Farrington herself most disliked. If the two of them were staying in London, however, Vivian felt that Ardmore Hall might suit her very well. She would at least have a reprieve from their everlasting carping and an opportunity to consider her problem.

"That is an excellent idea!" Lord Farrington nodded at his wife approvingly.

He turned to face Vivian. "You need a firm hand, young lady—not only from us, but from your husband. After you spend a few days alone at Ardmore Hall, I daresay my brother's company will be much more acceptable to you."

At the thought of having Lanyon inflicted upon her once more, Vivian's temper flared.

"Mr. Lanyon's company will *never* be acceptable to me!" she informed him. "Nor will I have his company forced upon me at Ardmore Hall—or anywhere else, for that matter!"

"You will do precisely as you are told!" he retorted, rising abruptly from the table. "You may expect to leave for Ardmore Hall tomorrow morning, miss!"

He turned on his heel and strode from the room, satisfied with his morning's work, and Lady Farrington followed in his wake, sparing not even a glance for her stepdaughter.

Vivian stared at her toast, her appetite gone. They planned to isolate her at Ardmore Hall and send Paul Lanyon there. There would be no escape for her in such a situation. Lord Farrington appeared very determined to keep her fortune in the family—but she was just as determined not to allow such a thing to befall her.

Chapter 4

The morning brought two other surprises. One was a letter delivered by hand to Vivian. Startled, she accepted it from one of the footmen, who explained when questioned that it had not been delivered with the morning post but had been brought by a messenger. When she saw the familiar handwriting and the seal on the wafer of wax, she had to hold back an exclamation of joy.

The second surprise, although not as exciting, was pleasant, nonetheless—and it provided her a temporary respite from the combined threat of Ardmore Hall and Paul Lanyon. A maid appeared in Vivian's chamber to inform her that she had a caller, and she most reluctantly went down to the drawing room. Paul Lanyon was the only person she could imagine her caller might be, and seeing him was scarcely what she had in mind.

Before she stepped into the drawing room, however, she straightened her shoulders and took a deep breath. She would not give him the satisfaction of knowing that he made her most uncomfortable. Instead, she would use this meeting to tell him very clearly how she felt about ever seeing him again.

So prepared was she to meet him that it took a moment for her to realize that there was no gentleman in the room. Lady Farrington rose from her chair and turned a glowing face toward her stepdaughter.

"Just see who has come to call, Vivian," she said brightly. "Lady Jersey has been so gracious as to call upon us and deliver your voucher to you personally! Lady Jersey, pray allow me to present my stepdaughter, Vivian Woodruff."

Vivian curtsied in response, as an elegantly dressed woman turned toward her and scrutinized her carefully.

"I understand, Miss Woodman, that you experienced quite an—active evening," said Lady Jersey.

"Woodruff," murmured Lady Farrington.

Lady Jersey favored her with an arctic glance, and Lady Farrington sank into silence.

Vivian nodded in agreement. "I did, indeed, Lady Jersey." She ventured nothing more, deciding that safety lay in saying as little as possible. Lady Farrington, however, having given up the matter of Vivian's proper name, wished to make her own position upon Vivian's abominable behavior quite clear—but she wished to do so without having the voucher revoked.

"She is very young, Lady Jersey," she said apologetically. "That must be her excuse."

Lady Jersey sniffed, apparently indicating disagreement. "If Anthony Mallory were to tempt me to go astray, Lady Farrington, I assure you that I should do so in an instant. You must know what a charming man he can be when he chooses."

Lady Farrington, who knew no such thing, found herself suddenly at sea. She had thought that they were discussing the matter of the infamous glass of claret, but the waltz appeared to have outweighed it in importance.

"I do not know Mr. Mallory," she ventured, her tone making it clear that she had no desire to know him.

Lady Jersey looked at her pityingly. "I can scarcely fault your daughter—no, your stepdaughter, is she not?" she corrected herself, seeing Lady Farrington's look of dismay. "I do not know any woman of taste who could say no to him, so how could I find fault with Miss Woodward?"

"Woodruff," murmured Lady Farrington once again, unable to stop herself. "But a young girl has no business at all standing up with him for a waltz, Lady Jersey. Surely you agree."

Vivian glanced at her stepmother. She was very eager to make a good impression on Lady Jersey and for Vivian to receive a voucher to Almack's—as proof of her own social prominence, of course—but she obviously still could not bear to let her stepdaughter off scot-free for her unladylike behavior.

"Of course I do not," Lady Jersey assured her. "It is more than obvious, Lady Farrington, that what you say is true and that you have no personal experience with Anthony Mallory."

Lady Farrington flushed and sat a little straighter. "Naturally I do not! Women of reputation do not allow themselves to be seen with a man that is known for eloping with the wives of other men or taking advantage of hapless men at the gaming table!"

Vivian's eyes widened slightly, both at the deeds attributed to Mr. Mallory and at Lady Farrington's reference to "women of reputation." It appeared to her to slight Lady Jersey. She saw, however, that Lady Jersey appeared amused by the comments.

"Don't worry, Lady Farrington," she said consolingly. "If he has not yet paid court to you, perhaps he will do so soon. After all, he has already taken note of your stepdaughter."

Lady Farrington turned scarlet at this comment and turned abruptly toward Vivian. She seemed, for the moment at least, not to be mindful of the impression she was making on Lady Jersey.

"Perhaps you should thank Lady Jersey once more and then go upstairs," she said shortly. "You will need to change your gown if we are to pay our own calls."

"I shall look forward to seeing you at Almack's tomorrow night, Miss Wooding," said Lady Jersey, who had stood at Lady Farrington's words. She smiled at Vivian, but she nodded toward Lady Farrington with a distant, distinctly chilly courtesy.

Vivian, mystified, made her curtsy to Lady Jersey and took herself upstairs. She had not known that she and her stepmother were planning to pay any calls, but she was relieved to be going out in company once more. And she was doubly relieved that she would be going to Almack's, for that guaranteed she would be staying in the city for at least a few days longer. It would be far better, she thought, to encounter Paul Lanyon in the midst of a group than it would be to have him forced upon her in the privacy of Ardmore Hall.

She felt far more cheerful than she had the night before. Not only had she received the unexpected letter and the respite from Ardmore Hall and Mr. Lanyon, but a glimmering of an idea had occurred to her—one that would rid her of her problem completely. Paul Lanyon and her stepparents would no longer be millstones about her neck.

She examined the idea, first from one perspective, then from another. It seemed to her that it would work quite well. Her future began to look much brighter. She would, at last, become a free woman.

Smiling, she changed her gown and did her hair. At last, she had discovered an escape—and the perfect vengeance. Her stepparents would undoubtedly sever all ties with her once she married Anthony Mallory. They would want nothing to do with a rakehell whose misdeeds constituted many of the latest *on-dits* of the *ton*, for Lord Farrington was a stickler for reputation. Lady Farrington, who had been somewhat more liberal in her views, had adopted his after their marriage.

Since Vivian's arrival in London, she had heard Anthony Mallory credited—or discredited—with running away with the wife of a well-known lord, with the destruction of another lord's family fortune at the gaming table, and even, it was whispered, with a duel that had resulted in the near death of the dishonored husband. She had heard Lord Farrington say that no gentleman with an ounce of self-respect would allow a female of his family near such a rogue.

Anthony Mallory would, Vivian thought with satisfaction, do very nicely as a husband. Her marriage to him would effectively remove her and her fortune beyond the reach of Lord and Lady Farrington. Of course, Mr. Mallory was not yet aware that he was about to marry her—but she was certain that he would do so.

After all, she had information that she knew he did not wish made public.

Chapter 5

After Vivian and Lady Farrington were settled in the carriage, Vivian turned to her stepmother.

"Well, Rebecca," she said, "just where are we going? I had not realized that we had plans, aside from tonight's ball."

"We are going to see Paul," she replied shortly, giving her attention to the passing scene. "I can see that you think that you are being rewarded for your behavior. Lady Jersey mentioned nothing except your dancing with Anthony Mallory, as though that was your only regrettable action last night."

Vivian stared at her, stunned by her words. "You cannot mean what you are saying, Rebecca! Why on earth would I call upon Mr. Lanyon? What possible purpose do you think that could serve?"

"You will apologize to him for your unladylike behavior," Lady Farrington replied. "And you will tell him that you will dance with him tonight."

She did not meet her stepdaughter's eyes, but instead continued to stare out the carriage window.

"I will do no such thing, Rebecca," responded Vivian, her voice firm. "I shall not even get out of the carriage when we arrive. You may do as you please, of course, but I shall remain where I am."

Lady Farrington shrugged. "Then I will bring him out to the carriage," she said indifferently. "Perhaps if the two of you take a ride alone, you will be more amenable."

Vivian said nothing more as the carriage rolled to a halt in front of the house where Paul Lanyon resided. A footman helped Lady Farrington from the carriage and closed the door behind her when Vivian remained seated. The two ladies did not even exchange a glance, but as soon as the butler had closed the door behind her stepmother, Vivian opened the carriage door and sprang lightly to the pavement.

"You may tell Lady Farrington that the day is so attractive that I decided to walk," she called to the driver and footman. Then she set off briskly down the street, determined to be out of sight by the time her stepmother and Lanyon returned to the carriage. The street was a busy one, but she turned the next corner and hurried past the busy shops, even though she wished to stop and look.

Once she had put several blocks and several turns between herself and the others, Vivian turned into an arcade and allowed herself the luxury of browsing through several small shops. She was glad that she had had the forethought to tuck some money into her reticule before leaving the house, and she emerged from the arcade with two new pairs of gloves and a fan. Pleased with herself for having so neatly evaded her stepmother and having given herself an unaccustomed outing at the same time, she set forth for home. She walked briskly, not minding either the distance or that she was unattended.

So absorbed was she in her own thoughts that she did not at first hear her name, but finally she became aware that a curricle had drawn up alongside her.

"Miss Woodruff, has something happened to your carriage?" repeated Mr. Mallory, looking down at her in concern. It was far from customary for a young lady to be walking unattended, carrying her own packages.

"No," she said cheerfully. "I abandoned it."

A look of amusement rippled across his dark face. "Indeed? Then I must assume it was behaving badly."

She nodded emphatically. "Most certainly it was. It insisted upon taking me someplace I had no wish to go, so I had no choice but to leave it."

He nodded. "I believe that right is on your side, Miss Woodruff. May I offer you a ride in my curricle if I swear that it will carry you nowhere save where you wish to be taken?"

Vivian appeared to consider the matter carefully and finally nodded judiciously. "I should like to be taken home, please," she said, allowing him to help her into the curricle and giving him her direction.

"Lady Jersey came to call on us this morning," she informed him. "Thank you, Mr. Mallory."

"For what?" he inquired, giving his attention to the traffic.

"For convincing her to give me a voucher for Almack's," Vivian replied.

"My congratulations, Miss Woodruff. I am certain that she was already planning to offer you one," he assured her.

"I doubt that, sir, so once again, I thank you."

He glanced at her and nodded, then looked back at the busy street through which they were threading their way.

She had never ridden in a curricle before, and certainly she had never ridden with someone who handled the ribbons as deftly as Mr. Mallory did. She gave herself over to the enjoyment of the ride, for she knew it would be a brief one.

When they reached Lord Farrington's home, Mallory sprang down to assist her from the curricle. She gave him her hand and stepped down carefully. Her hand was very small in his, and she had a fleeting feeling of security that was very foreign to her. He was, she thought, a much more comfortable man than she imagined a rogue would be.

"Thank you, Mr. Mallory. It was very kind of you to come to my rescue once more," she said, smiling up at him.

"I do wish, Miss Woodruff, that you would stop describing me as kind," he complained, returning her smile. "You will ruin my reputation."

"Will you be at Lady Belvedere's ball tonight?" she asked, thinking once again of her plan.

"If you are to be there, naturally I must be also," he replied gallantly, bowing to her.

Vivian chuckled. "I am glad to know that you were already planning to go, whether I appeared or not."

"Do you doubt my sincerity, Miss Woodruff?" he demanded, assuming an injured air. "Come tonight and I shall dance every dance with you."

"And then I would be right back in the same predicament," she pointed out, "since young ladies are not supposed to dance with a gentleman more than twice. You would once again be obliged to rescue me."

He sighed deeply. "Then I suppose I must confine myself to two dances, Miss Woodruff," he conceded. "But I insist that I must have the first one."

"If I am allowed to attend, you may surely have it," she assured him.

He frowned. "Is there some doubt about your attendance?"

"I must have permission, you see," she told him. "And if my stepparents are too displeased with me, then I may be compelled to stay at home this evening—but if I cannot come, sir, would you do me a favor?"

"Anything," he assured her, although he was watching her with a wary eye. He had seen her in action and was aware that her favor might be difficult to do.

"I am certain that we will be at Almack's tomorrow evening because Lady Farrington wishes to go, and she would not wish to offend Lady Jersey by not allowing me to attend also. Will you come to Almack's?"

Almack's was among the places that Anthony Mallory least wished to go. Few gentlemen, particularly those still young and lively, cared for the staid and stuffy Almack's. The atmosphere was dull, the refreshments bland, and the gambling stakes low.

Mallory looked down at her small, intent face and sighed. "If you wish for me to do so, Miss Woodruff, then naturally I must," he replied.

Once again he wondered what in heaven's name possessed him to agree, but he was discovering that he found it difficult to deny her anything. Such a situation could be, he knew, most dangerous. He would be wise to remove himself from Miss Woodruff's vicinity as soon as possible.

She smiled at him. "I can see that you have no desire to go to Almack's, Mr. Mallory. But I assure you that, if you attend, I shall have a surprise for you."

His eyebrows lifted. "A surprise? What sort of surprise, miss?" he inquired.

"I will tell you then," Vivian responded. "But I promise you that you would never guess what it is, not if you guessed for a thousand years."

"I am intrigued, Miss Woodruff," he said—and, to his surprise, he was. Although easily bored and considering himself quite jaded, during the past twenty-four hours he had found himself thinking very often of the young lady before him. "If you are not at Lady Belvedere's ball tonight, I swear that I shall be at Almack's tomorrow night."

It would be soon enough to take himself out of harm's way after that meeting, he thought. After all, what damage could possibly be done during an evening an Almack's?

Satisfied, Vivian took her packages from Mr. Mallory and ran lightly up the steps to the front door. Turning, she smiled and waved to him before going in.

Things could not have been going better, she thought, very pleased with the events of the day.

Just as she had suspected, her angry stepmother informed her that she would not be attending Lady Belvedere's ball and that she could, instead, sit at home alone and meditate upon her ungrateful behavior.

Grateful to be at least left alone instead of in company with Mr. Lanyon, she did, indeed, stay at home and meditate, but not upon her sins. Instead, she considered very carefully what she would do at Almack's on the following night. Lady Farrington, who smiled when she saw Mallory glance in her direction that night, obviously looking for Vivian, would have been far less satisfied with the punishment she had meted out had she known what her stepdaughter was planning.

Chapter 6

Anthony Mallory glanced at the throng surrounding him at Almack's and wondered again what had possessed him when he agreed to come tonight. He was dressed in the mandatory knee breeches, which he detested, and as he surveyed the huge ballroom in which he stood, he could see no one with whom he wished to speak. He knew that many were amazed he was accepted inside the doors of this formidably respectable club, but he had long been a favorite of most of the patronesses. He briefly considered retiring to inspect the refreshments, but a moment's reflection kept him from it. The food would be deplorable and the drinks insipid, so he might just as well stand and wait for Miss Woodruff to appear. After dancing with her and being apprised of her surprise, he would take himself away to clubs that were far more to his taste.

Vivian entered shortly thereafter, and he watched her entrance with appreciation. Lady Farrington was unquestionably a beautiful woman still, but

her stepdaughter outshone her because of the an-
imation of her face and her movement. Lady
Farrington, in comparison, looked as though she
were only half alive. Lord Farrington escorted
them, and Mallory saw Paul Lanyon making his
way toward them.

That spurred him into action, and he bore
down upon Miss Woodruff before either of her
stepparents saw him coming and had the opportunity to prepare themselves. Their startled expressions showed that they most certainly had not
expected to encounter him at Almack's, of all
places. Within moments, he had deftly separated
Miss Woodruff from them and led her onto the
dance floor.

"You were just in time," Vivian said gratefully,
nodding in the general direction of Mr. Lanyon. "I
was afraid that I would have to begin my evening
with him."

"I am pleased to see that they allowed you out
this evening, Miss Woodruff," he told her. "I was
beginning to fear that I had attired myself in this
regalia only to stand about for an hour or two, sip-
ping ratafia and fighting off boredom of monu-
mental proportions."

Vivian laughed, and he was charmed once more
to see that her laugh was real and that it lit up her
dark eyes. She seemed to him to have little of the
flirt about her, but her warmth and humor acted
like a magnet for him. She was, he thought, most
charming, and he was willing to undergo even the
rigors of Almack's for her—at least for an hour or
two on this single occasion.

"I do apologize, Mr. Mallory. I know that this is
scarcely how you would like to spend your evening,
but I do so appreciate your coming."

"I have no quarrel with my suffering now that you have come, Miss Woodruff," he assured her. "Your presence makes even Almack's seem acceptable."

She held her head to one side, rather like a small, bright-eyed bird, and studied him for a moment before replying. "I can see why you are a favorite of the ladies, sir. Such attention is as heady as any wine."

"But sincere, Miss Woodruff—I do not say what I do not mean. I never offer false coin."

"And I believe you, sir—a fact that must be a tribute to how polished a flirt you are."

He did not respond for a moment, and the movement of the dance separated them. When he joined her once more, he looked at her curiously.

"Are you not at least a little afraid of me, Miss Woodruff?" he asked. "I know you must be aware of my reputation. I am certain that Lady Farrington made that very clear to you."

"I have, indeed, heard things about you, Mr. Mallory, although I naturally do not know that they are true."

"And if I told you that they were all true? That I had, indeed, done everything that has been attributed to me? What would you say then?"

Vivian paused and then shook her head. "It would not matter. I feel comfortable with you, Mr. Mallory, so how could I be afraid?"

Mallory shook his head. "You are very young, miss. Too young perhaps to be afraid—and certainly too young to be wise in the ways of the world."

"Are you warning me away, Mr. Mallory?" Vivian asked. Although his voice was still light, he seemed to have grown more serious about what he was saying. "Are you telling me that I should be afraid of you?"

He shrugged. "Perhaps," he admitted. "Perhaps you should listen to your stepmother."

Vivian laughed—but without mirth. "My stepmother wishes me to marry Paul Lanyon. How can I listen to her? I cannot imagine a more miserable existence than the one that she wishes for me."

"You need not marry Lanyon, Miss Woodruff. They cannot force you to do so, and there are many others from whom you could choose a husband."

They separated once more, and when they came together once more, Vivian murmured to him, "If you look to your left, sir, you will see my stepmother's reaction to our dancing together."

A single glance told the tale. Lady Farrington's face appeared frozen, and she kept her eyes fixed upon Vivian. If Vivian's reception at home after waltzing with Mr. Mallory and tossing wine on Mr. Lanyon had been unpleasant, tonight's promised to surpass it in intensity. Mallory wondered uneasily if he was once again placing her in an indefensible position.

When the dance ended, he led her to one side and spoke in a low voice. "Perhaps we should not dance another time, Miss Woodruff. There is no need to anger her more—doing so will only make life more difficult for you."

Vivian shook her head. "It is already difficult, Mr. Mallory. And I still need to speak with you, whether we dance together again or not."

He nodded, deciding that it might be best to do that immediately. He could see that Lady Farrington had turned in their direction and would undoubtedly seek them out as soon as she could. He took Vivian's arm and steered her through the throng, hoping to find a relatively quiet spot and to put some distance between them and Lady Farrington.

"Now, Miss Woodruff," he said, keeping his voice low and promising himself to keep the exchange very brief, "just how may I be of service to you?"

Vivian did not miss a beat. "I wish for you to marry me, Mr. Mallory," she said, looking him in the eye as she spoke. "Will you do so?"

For a moment, Mallory felt as though someone had just struck the backs of his knees and feared they might buckle beneath him. He understood then just why ladies prone to fainting spells carried smelling salts with them.

He cleared his throat tentatively, wishing for the bracing fumes of some sal volatile. "I beg your pardon, Miss Woodruff. Perhaps I did not understand you properly—"

She smiled at him. "You understood me perfectly well, Mr. Mallory. You simply do not wish to answer me."

"May I ask *why* you wish to marry me, Miss Woodruff? I cannot convince myself that you found me so irresistible upon our first meeting that you determined then that I was the only man you wished to marry."

Vivian smiled. "Do you have no belief in *Romeo and Juliet* then, sir? No belief in love at first sight?"

"I have loved *several* times at first sight, so you must understand that I do not place great faith in it," he replied, "and I am certain that you felt no such attraction to me when you were rinsing Mr. Lanyon's waistcoat in claret. I was simply your escape route—which I was delighted to be, of course."

Vivian nodded. "You were, indeed, my escape,"

she agreed, "and I should like for you to provide for my escape once more."

"By *marrying* you?" he demanded, still keeping his voice low, although it was growing in intensity. "I cannot see why you would consider marriage an escape."

"That is because no one is pressing you to marry Paul Lanyon," she returned. "You would see things quite differently if you were to find yourself in such a situation."

"Undoubtedly I would feel quite differently about it under those circumstances," he replied, a smile creasing his face at her explanation. "But, as I told you, Miss Woodruff—although they can make life unpleasant for you, they cannot force you to marry him."

Vivian fixed him with a steady gaze. "They can send me away to Ardmore Hall alone and then send him there to keep me company. They can isolate me so that I have contact with no one else. You know that they have that power, Mr. Mallory."

His certainty faltered. "But you have only to remain resolute, Miss Woodruff—and I am quite certain that you can do that. You have only to tell him and your stepmother that you will not marry Lanyon."

"I have no wish to be held a virtual prisoner in my own home, Mr. Mallory. Why should I have to suffer such treatment? If I marry, neither my stepmother nor her husband will have any power over me or my fortune. And you and I need not remain married, of course—it would simply be a convenient connection to protect me."

Mallory cleared his throat with what could have been mistaken for a nervous cough. He did not wish Miss Woodruff to be subjected to ill treatment, of course—the very thought was abominable—but he had no wish to marry, either.

Vivian could see that clearly, and she shook her head. "I can see that you intend to refuse my request," she sighed, "so I am forced to say something to you that I had hoped to avoid."

Mallory looked at her apprehensively. He was a man accustomed to being in control of every situation, but his world seemed to have slipped slightly askew in the last few minutes. In fact, he felt as though everything had gone topsy-turvy. He would not have been surprised if Miss Woodruff next announced that she wished for him to challenge Farrington or Lanyon to a duel. He would not put it past her for a moment.

"And what would that be?" he asked cautiously.

"Lady Luxley," she responded. "Lady Luxley and Brexton Manor."

He stared at her in disbelief, and his dark face grew even darker. Any faint amusement he might have felt at the situation vanished in an instant. "What do you mean by that, Miss Woodruff?" he asked, his tone forbidding.

For a moment Vivian felt a ripple of apprehension. She could see no friendliness or amusement in his face now—quite the opposite, in fact.

"I don't need to explain it for you, sir," she said firmly, determined not to allow her voice to quiver, for his abrupt change in manner had struck her forcibly. "You understand me."

"No," he said, shaking his head slowly, "I am not certain that I do. Exactly what do you want me to understand by your cryptic mention of a person and a place?"

"That I know you have her hidden there," replied Vivian in a voice scarcely above a whisper, "and that you would naturally not wish anyone—particularly Lord Luxley—to know of her whereabouts."

At that, Mallory's hand shot out and gripped her arm so tightly that she almost cried out. She had read stories in which the eyes of the characters were said to blaze with anger, but she had never before seen that fire in the eyes of a real person. When he bent toward her, she leaned as far away from him as she possibly could. For the first time she doubted the wisdom of her plan.

"That sounded very much like a threat, Miss Woodruff!" His voice was still low, so very low that it sounded much like a growl.

"No, no, of course not," she hastened to assure him, but her words sounded weak, even to her.

"Then what—*exactly* what—do you mean?" he demanded.

Vivian wondered what had ever made her think that she was comfortable with this man. Her overpowering thought was that she should get away from him as quickly as possible.

Then, across the room, she saw Paul Lanyon, and she squared her shoulders and faced the wrath of Anthony Mallory.

"I mean that you wish to keep her whereabouts a secret and I wish to help you to do so," she said, keeping her voice as firm as she could manage.

They were able to say no more because at that moment Lady Farrington arrived, having finally managed to run them to earth.

"Vivian!" she said sharply. "You are to dance the quadrille with Paul, and then Lady Jersey wishes to speak with you." She took Vivian firmly in hand and towed her along, sparing not even a glance for Mr. Mallory.

As Vivian looked back over her shoulder and caught a glimpse of his face, she was certain of one thing: Mr. Mallory had not finished the conversation about Lady Luxley and their marriage.

That was what she had wanted, of course, but she shuddered slightly. She had not thought his reaction would be like this—not so very nearly a violent one. And she had been persuaded that she knew him and rather liked him.

Now she wondered if she would be leaping from the frying pan into the fire by marrying him.

Chapter 7

True to her word, Lady Farrington steered her relentlessly toward Mr. Lanyon. Despite her distress after the encounter with Mr. Mallory, Vivian could scarcely repress a smile at the sight of Paul Lanyon's face as they approached. He scarcely looked the part of the eager lover. He looked, instead, more like a rabbit cornered by a hunter, knowing that the seconds of its life were numbered. If he had more backbone, she reflected, he would tell his brother that he had no wish to marry a woman who would throw things at him and embarrass him in public.

But then, of course, there was the question of her fortune. She supposed that Mr. Lanyon was willing to undergo a certain amount of distress in order to gain control of it. And once they were married, he would be free to discipline her wayward manners as he thought best. The law gave him every right to do so and accorded her no redress. As her thoughts progressed down this unpleasant path, Vivian shuddered, and all amusement at the situation left her.

The matter was serious—and she had no intention of allowing herself to be ordered about or of having her life decided by others. Mr. Mallory would be more than willing to order her about, naturally, but she knew that he had no wish to marry her and would have their legal connection dissolved so that he could be rid of her as soon as was humanly possible.

As she began the dance with Lanyon, she caught sight of Mr. Mallory once more. She had expected him to leave in a fit of anger, for obviously it would be almost impossible for them to speak again that evening. His eyes were fixed upon her, however, and his gaze was anything but loverlike. She shivered slightly, feeling his disapproval sweep across her like a wave. It was surprising, she thought, that it should matter to her at all what a virtual stranger thought of her. She had enjoyed his indulgent amusement, certain that he regarded very few people with the sort of absent affection he had shown her. She had felt—for want of a better word—safe when she was with him, and she regretted the loss of that feeling.

Mr. Lanyon was also eyeing her, but with a very different emotion. He was watching her cautiously, as though fearful that she was carrying a glass of claret hidden upon her person, planning to sweep it out and drench him when he least expected it. For a moment she toyed with the possibility of marrying him, wondering if she would then be able to rule the household and her husband. She discarded the thought quickly, however. Not only was it distasteful, but she was quite certain that it was inaccurate as well. Even in her brief life, she had had occasion to note that weak men often became tyrants in their own households, determined to show mastery somewhere.

She smiled at Lanyon pleasantly—or at least she hoped it was pleasantly. "Was your valet able to remove the wine stain?" she inquired innocently.

Mr. Lanyon immediately looked more wary still. "No—that is, not all of it, I fear," he said stiffly.

She clucked sympathetically. "Well, as Mr. Mallory was so quick to point out, red wine does unfortunately stain quickly and often permanently."

Her partner showed the faintest trace of color in his cheeks. "It seems to me, Vivian—Miss Woodruff," he hastened to make the change, almost tripping over one of the other dancers as he did so, "that you should be apologizing for that episode. I understood from Lady Farrington that you regretted your action and wished to tell me so."

"Indeed?" replied Vivian politely. "I fear that my stepmother was mistaken, sir. She very often makes the error of believing that she can do my thinking for me."

The dance led them to other partners, but when she rejoined him, he took up the conversation again.

"Do you mean to say that you do not regret destroying an expensive waistcoat and creating a scene that embarrassed us both?" he asked, careful to keep his voice low and Vivian at a safe distance.

Vivian nodded, smiling as sweetly as though she were agreeing that the weather had, indeed, been fine that day. "You have stated the matter very well, sir," she said approvingly. "I have no regrets at all about that occurrence."

"Gentlemen wish for their wives to be ladies, Miss Woodruff, behaving in a modest, becoming manner," he said indignantly.

"And we are all free to wish what we choose," replied Vivian, nodding. "I, for instance, do not wish to be ordered about or manhandled as though I were a spaniel being trained for the hunt."

Mr. Lanyon squared his narrow shoulders and stood as tall as he could manage, attempting to look imposing. "Clearly, Lady Farrington is correct when she says that your father indulged you and made you unfit to be a wife."

Again, Vivian nodded serenely. "I am most certainly unfit to be *your* wife, Mr. Lanyon. I am pleased that you have also reached that conclusion."

"I fear we have reached two different conclusions, miss," he said, bowing stiffly as the dance ended. "I have concluded that we would be well suited once we are married and I have taught you the proper manners."

"And I have concluded, sir, that you will never have that opportunity," Vivian replied sweetly, curtsying to him and then turning on her heel and walking away.

Anthony Mallory had seen this interchange, having watched Vivian during the whole of the dance. If she were correct, he reflected, and she was to be married off to Lanyon despite her own wishes, then perhaps he might be justified if he intervened. The girl was obviously determined to ruin herself one way or another, and he was not going to stand by and allow her to sacrifice Lady Luxley to her foolish attempts to force him into marriage. No doubt he would regret what he was about to do, but it would at least spare Diana, and Miss Woodruff would be no worse off than she would be were she to become Mrs. Paul Lanyon, a fate that Mallory had to agree would be decidedly unpleasant.

Vivian had been careful to direct her steps away

from Mr. Mallory, for she had no desire to speak with him again until she had had the opportunity to order her thoughts. Just a few minutes would enable her to do that, she felt certain, and then she would be forced to address the matter of Lady Luxley once more, no matter how distasteful it was to her—and no matter whether she dreaded seeing Mr. Mallory's reaction. She had no choice.

She was not pleased, therefore, to hear him speak to her as she made her way into one of the large side rooms where refreshments were served. She turned to look at him, knowing that her expression must be fully as wary as Mr. Lanyon's had been when he looked at her. The comparison had no power to amuse her, however.

"Yes, Mr. Mallory?" she said cautiously. His expression, she saw, was tightly controlled. Whatever anger he felt had been banked, and his eyes were cold.

"I have considered your suggestion, miss," he said, his voice devoid of any emotion whatsoever, "and I have decided that I will help you."

Vivian's heart leapt at his words, for she had not expected him to give way so quickly.

"Thank you, Mr. Mallory," she replied fervently. "You will not regret it."

He studied her for a moment before answering. "I hope that you are correct, Miss Woodruff—but since I have someone to protect, I have very little choice, as you well know."

Vivian flushed uncomfortably. "I have no wish to harm, sir. I hope that you believe me when I say that."

"We shall see," he said briefly. "You may be assured that I will allow no harm to come to her."

A threat was implicit in his words, but Vivian did

not react to it with anger. She bowed her head and nodded. It was only to be expected that he would protect the woman he loved by any means available to him, and she could not think less of him for doing so.

"Are you able to leave your home at night without being detected?" he asked abruptly.

Vivian nodded, suddenly nervous.

"Very well." He removed a gold watch from his pocket and glanced down at it. "I will be waiting in front of your house in four hours time."

Vivian could not restrain a gasp. "Why?"

Mr. Mallory looked at her in surprise. "You wish to escape your family, do you not?"

She nodded.

"Then you will meet me at that time, Miss Woodruff." And he turned and disappeared into the crowd.

Stunned, Vivian wondered just what trouble she had brought upon herself. Her plan seemed to be working all too well.

Chapter 8

It was very dark when she unbarred the front door and slipped quietly out. Despite her dislike for her stepparents, she trusted that no one would rob them while the door was unlocked—and that none of the servants would be dismissed for leaving it that way. That, she knew, would be the first conclusion the butler would draw when he saw it unbarred. She was comforted to think that the dismissal would not last long, even if it occurred, because when they discovered that she was gone, the matter of the door would be explained.

Mr. Mallory stepped out of the dark closed carriage and helped her into it. The carriage lamps were not lit, and not until they had traveled almost a mile did the driver stop to light them.

"By the time Lady Farrington realizes that you are gone, we will have several hours head start," he said with satisfaction. "They will not be able to find us easily, if at all."

"But surely they will be able to catch up with us before we reach Gretna Green," Vivian protested.

The Scottish border was, after all, a long distance away, and it was well known as the favorite destination for runaway marriages. English law prohibited the marriage of a minor without parental consent, but Scotland had no such law.

"But we are not going to Gretna Green," he replied.

There was a pause while Vivian considered his words. "We are going to Scotland, are we not?" she asked, thinking of marriage.

"No, we are not," said Mallory.

A longer pause followed, and then Vivian asked hesitantly, "Then where are we going, sir?"

"Why, to Brexton Manor, of course," he replied smoothly, wondering what her reaction would be.

The pause that then ensued lasted a very long time, indeed. Vivian's head was whirling. They were going to Brexton Manor! As she considered the matter, her heart lightened. It would not solve her problem, of course, but it would, indeed, give her time away from Lord and Lady Farrington while she considered her options, and she would see Louisa again! And an additional bonus was that for the time being she would not be married to anyone. She was, in fact, delightfully—if only temporarily—free!

"Brexton Manor! How splendid!" she sighed. Then, a great weight taken from her shoulders, she promptly fell asleep.

Anthony Mallory frowned. Why would she think that going to Brexton Manor was splendid? he asked himself. That had certainly formed no part of her plan. He was quite certain that she had come only because she believed that they would be eloping to Scotland. When he told her their destination, he had expected tears and recrimination, not pleasure and relief. He might have suspected that she was acting, just to show that she was in control of herself and the situation, except that she was undeniably fast asleep, her breathing low and even.

Just what he would do with Miss Woodruff when he reached Brexton Manor, he had no idea. And he did not think that Lady Luxley would be likely to approve of someone else being admitted into their secret without consulting her. He sighed and stared out the window at the shadowy landscape rolling by them. Once again he had to ask himself what had possessed him to become embroiled with a troublesome schoolgirl who had attempted to blackmail him. Doubtless Diana would point that out to him, too, and he would have no satisfactory answer—except perhaps that he had suffered a brief period of lunacy.

The journey to Brexton Manor was far to the north, and they reached it without incident. They had stopped twice along the way to change horses and to eat, although Vivian had slept through the first stop. Feeling that she was at least temporarily safe had apparently enabled her to sleep more soundly than she had been able to for weeks. Even when she awakened at the second stop and went into the inn to eat, she had had little to say and had promptly gone back to sleep the instant she returned to the carriage.

They arrived at their destination after Lady Luxley had retired, but Mallory had given Vivian over to the care of his housekeeper, who escorted her up to a guest chamber and helped her prepare for bed. That required little enough, for the girl tumbled into bed as soon as she was in her nightgown. Mallory, on the other hand, sat long before his fire that evening, wondering just how to handle

all of the feminine problems that had fallen his lot
to solve.

He had by no means reached any conclusions
by the time he faced Lady Luxley the next morning after breakfast. She entered the library, looking as lovely as she always did, chestnut hair
glowing in the morning sun that shone in bright
shafts across the room.

"Anthony, how delightful that you have come!"
She crossed the room toward him, and he stood,
folding her in his arms and hugging her.

Vivian had awakened early, rested by her thirty
minutes of sleep, dressed, and made her way quietly downstairs. She had seen Lady Luxley cross
the hall into the library, and she had stolen down
the stairs to stand at the open door, feeling like an
interloper.

Lady Luxley stood back from him and cupped
his face in her hands. "You look dreadfully tired,
Anthony. What is it? Mrs. Mellon told me that you
arrived here with a schoolgirl. What has happened?"

Vivian's cheeks burned. She was, of course, little
more than a schoolgirl, but it still rankled to hear
herself described in such a manner. She had
thought that she had acquired at least a little town
bronze during her fortnight in London, but it was
obvious that Mrs. Mellon had not noticed it.

Mallory's tone was apologetic when he spoke.
"She was in trouble, Diana, and I could not think
of anywhere else to take her."

"In trouble? What sort of trouble?" asked Lady
Luxley.

"Her stepmother is trying to force her into a
marriage that she does not wish—indeed, she was

desperate enough to try to convince me to elope with her."

Lady Luxley laughed, the same gentle, infectious laugh that Vivian loved. She had no trouble at all understanding why Mr. Mallory loved her.

"She must certainly have been desperate, Anthony, if she wished to elope with you." She paused a moment, thinking it over. "Did you bring her here alone, Anthony? Unchaperoned?"

Mallory looked uncomfortable and nodded, knowing that trouble was brewing.

Lady Luxley shook her head. "You should not have done so, Anthony. You know that a scandal such as this can ruin a young girl's reputation. What will her family tell people about what has happened? She will go home to scandal broth."

Mallory sighed and nodded. "That did, indeed, occur to me, Diana—but not until we were already on our way. I confess that I am seldom inclined to think of reputation."

Before Lady Luxley could reply, Vivian stood in the doorway and cleared her throat lightly. Both of them looked up, and Lady Luxley's eyes lighted with pleasure.

"Vivian!" she cried. "Are you the schoolgirl?"

Vivian ran across the room and into her waiting arms, grateful to be close to a friend at last.

"Has that dreadful woman been trying to force you into a marriage?" she demanded, holding Vivian's head against her shoulder.

Vivian nodded convulsively, her shoulders shaking. It was the most immense relief to tell her problem to someone she could trust. She knew that Lady Luxley would champion her cause and never question her word. It was sharply painful that she was also the love of Anthony Mallory's life, but at least she felt that he had made a worthy choice. She could no longer doubt the manner of man he was if he loved Louisa's mother.

"Is Louisa here?" Vivian asked, and Lady Luxley looked at her in surprise.

"No, Vivian. Why, were you expecting to find her here?"

Vivian flushed and glanced briefly at Mallory. "I was not supposed to tell anyone about it, but she wrote to me and told me where you were and that she was joining you here. I thought perhaps she might have arrived."

Mallory, seeing that his problem was growing more intricate by the moment, sighed and sat down. Despite the sigh, he smiled at Lady Luxley.

"Well, at least I know how Miss Woodruff discovered your presence here, Diana. That had me very worried. I feared that perhaps it had become widely known."

He glanced at Vivian. "I was going to question you about it on the journey here, but you slept the entire way."

Lady Luxley looked anxiously at them both, her voice serious when she spoke. "What I said about doing damage to a young girl's reputation still stands, Anthony—only now the matter is much more important because this is Vivian and not a stranger."

He nodded. "We will think of some way around it," he said. "We will have a little time to consider the matter."

Lady Luxley shook her head in disagreement. "Very little," she replied. "What is Lady Farrington going to think? Vivian, did you leave a note telling her that you were eloping, or did you just leave without any note at all, and allow them to think that you ran away?"

"I left a note," she replied. "I told them that I was eloping to Gretna Green." She glanced at Mallory. "But I did not mention any names."

Mallory shook his head. "I don't think that it will take them very long to arrive at a name, Miss Woodruff. All they have to do is to consider the events of the past few days. Then Farrington will make casual inquiries and discover that I left town hurriedly at the same time you disappeared."

Lady Luxley had regarded him with interest when he referred to the events of the past days, but she decided that she would inquire into that matter later.

"In any case," she said, "the news cannot be kept quiet for very long, and once it is known, Vivian will find herself at the center of a scandal."

"But I don't give a fig about that, Lady Luxley! Why should I care about that?"

"Because you will wish to marry, Vivian," she replied gravely, "and gentlemen often become quite particular about the reputations of their brides."

"Well, I shan't marry a man who doesn't believe me when I say I have nothing to be ashamed of!" Vivian exclaimed hotly. "And I should imagine that someone like that dreadful Paul Lanyon wouldn't care about my reputation so long as he got to manage my fortune!"

"He is the one that Lady Farrington wishes you to marry?" inquired Lady Luxley, smoothing Vivian's hair back from her face and patting her shoulder.

Vivian nodded. "He is a perfect horror! He is Lord Farrington's youngest brother, and they foist him upon me at every turn. He reminds me of nothing so much as a toad!"

Lady Luxley nodded sympathetically. "And you need not marry him, my dear."

"So I told her," said Mallory, "but she would not believe me."

"But if you would only have married me, Mr. Mallory—just for a few weeks, you understand—I could have been rid of them completely."

"You were very enterprising to think of that, Vivian," said Lady Luxley. "You have never been lacking in spirit."

"Don't encourage her, Diana," Mallory cautioned. "She was willing to blackmail me, using her knowledge of your presence here to force me to marry her."

Lady Luxley stared at her, and Vivian turned scarlet to the roots of her hair. "You know, Lady Luxley, that I would never, *never* in this life do anything to harm you!" she exclaimed, looking at her beseechingly. "But Mr. Mallory could not know that, and I knew that he would not allow your presence here to be known."

"Of course I know that you wouldn't harm me, Vivian," she responded, "but what made you think that you could use that information against Anthony?"

Vivian stared at her. "Well, everyone knows that you are the great love of his life, Lady Luxley. Naturally he would do anything for you."

Even as she said the words, Vivian felt the sharp pain of them. It seemed most unfair that she should find a gentleman she liked, only to discover not only that he was a rogue—which she could have accepted—but that he already loved someone else.

She stared down at her hands, now folded neatly

in her lap. "I was wrong to try to use that love, though. I realize that now. It was very selfish of me."

Before either of them could reply, a footman appeared in the doorway of the library.

"Mr. Mallory, you have callers, sir. Lord and Lady Farrington and a Mr. Lanyon."

An abrupt silence fell upon them, but it was broken almost instantly as the guests swept past the footman and into the library.

If a person can be said to swell with indignation, Lady Farrington did so when she entered the room and saw the three of them.

"So! Not only have you kidnapped my stepdaughter, Mr. Mallory, but you have brought her here to your love nest!" She glared at Lady Luxley. "And to think that I entrusted Vivian to your care so many times without knowing what manner of woman you were!"

"But I have always known what manner of woman you are, Lady Farrington," she responded calmly. "It is refreshing, though, to see you so concerned about Vivian's welfare. There have been a good many times when I would have sworn you did not even realize that you had a stepdaughter."

Lady Farrington appeared to swell to alarming proportions at these remarks, her cheeks puffing with indignation.

"My wife should not even be speaking to a woman who disregards her own good name and that of her husband," inserted Lord Farrington, who had been surveying everyone in the room with disapproval, and Mr. Lanyon, hovering in his brother's shadow, nodded his agreement.

"You should be very cautious how you speak of a lady's reputation," said Mallory, rising and walking slowly toward the gentlemen. His tone, Vivian noted with pleasure, was distinctly ominous. "Duels have been fought over such matters, as I am certain you know."

Mr. Lanyon edged farther into his brother's shadow, and Lord Farrington's Adam's apple grew visible as he swallowed.

As he neared his guests, Mr. Mallory spoke again, keeping his gaze firmly upon Lord Farrington.

"Why don't you apologize to Lady Luxley, sir?" he inquired gently. "I am certain that you spoke in the heat of the moment, without measuring your words properly. Am I correct?"

Lord Farrington paused a moment, then nodded slowly, with his shadow nodding right along with him. Lady Farrington once more appeared to swell, and Vivian had a sudden vision of what her stepmother would look like in another ten years. It cheered her immeasurably—almost as much as the scene that was unfolding before her.

"Well?" prodded Mallory gently, still watching Lord Farrington.

"If I have spoken out of turn, Lady Luxley—" he began, but Mr. Mallory shook his head and cut him short.

"Not 'if,' Lord Farrington. You did, indeed, speak out of turn. Do try again."

Lord Farrington swallowed once more and began again. "I spoke out of turn, Lady Luxley, and I regret anything offensive that I said to you."

Lady Luxley nodded pleasantly. "And I accept your apology, Lord Farrington."

Mr. Mallory turned his gaze upon Lady Farrington, and she gazed at him defiantly. "As for you, ma'am, since I do not fight duels with women, you are, of course, quite safe from me."

Vivian noticed with amusement that Mr. Lanyon looked at his sister-in-law as though jealous of the safety afforded her by her sex.

"However," he continued, "I do have a weapon that I can and will use against you, should you choose to abuse Lady Luxley again."

"Indeed?" asked Lady Farrington. "And what would that be, sir? Since it could not be a sword or a pistol, would you perhaps use a club against a mere woman?"

Lord Farrington, envisioning himself having to fight a duel on his wife's behalf, murmured to her to have a care about what she said, but she waved him away as she might a fly that was troubling her.

"Oh no, Lady Farrington," Mallory assured her. "The weapon is one you yourself would recognize and appreciate. It would require only a word from me into the ear of someone like—perhaps someone like Lady Jersey—suggesting that you have been defaming a dear friend of hers."

He paused and watched the effect of his words. She grew quite pale, thinking of the voucher that had arrived, personally presented by that lady. She had thought Lady Jersey's attentiveness a compliment to herself, but she made the proper connections now.

He nodded and smiled. "I can see that you understand, ma'am. I think I need say no more."

He turned to the whole group. "And now," he continued, "although we have several things of importance to discuss, I will have you shown to your rooms so that you may rest for a while and have some refreshments. I know that you must have traveled all night in order to reach here at this hour."

"If you think that we will stay under the same

roof—" began Lady Farrington, but her husband hurriedly stopped her.

"But of course we will, my dear," he assured her. "It is very kind of Mr. Mallory to invite us to stay."

Lady Farrington's mouth opened and closed several times as she looked at her runaway stepdaughter and the infamous Lady Luxley and Mr. Mallory. Vivian noted with interest that the fishlike tendencies appeared to be contagious, as well as hereditary, since she too was falling prey to them. And, although she disliked the idea of being under the same roof with Mr. Lanyon, she knew that with Mr. Mallory and Lady Luxley, she would not be troubled.

"However did they arrive here so quickly?" asked Lady Luxley once the new arrivals had been shown to their chambers.

Vivian shook her head. "One of the servants must have heard me unbolt the door. Or perhaps someone had a window open and looked out when they heard the carriage. Rest assured it was a servant, though. Neither of my stepparents would hear a thing, and they never sleep with their windows open."

"Still," protested Lady Luxley, "even if a servant heard the carriage and saw you get into it, how did they manage to follow it so swiftly? It would already have been out of sight by the time they could have had their own brought round, ready for the trip."

"That can probably be laid at my door," admitted Mallory as he considered the matter. "When my carriage was prepared for the journey, something could easily have been said in front of one of the boys that work in the stable where it is stored, and a guinea might have bought the information from them. And heaven knows their suspicions would have alighted immediately on me as the seducer of young virtue."

Lady Luxley shook her head. "Well, however they found Vivian, it is just as well that they did so. We will deal with the situation now, as quickly and cleanly as possible. Perhaps Vivian will emerge from this unscathed after all."

Vivian shrugged carelessly. "It does not matter, Lady Luxley. Pray do not concern yourself over it."

"Vivian," she replied, her voice edged with impatience, "you must believe me when I say that a day may come when you prize that reputation you are so eager to throw away."

Thinking of Lady Luxley's own situation, Vivian said no more on the subject, and a few minutes later she slipped out the French window that opened onto a garden. It was a lovely morning, all light and freshness and birdsong, and for a moment she felt happy, quite as though her world were in order—which, she reflected sadly, it most certainly was not.

To her surprise, Mr. Mallory joined her a few minutes later, guiding her toward a stone bench where they could sit and look out over the garden and a stretch of rolling hills. They sat in silence for a few minutes, but finally he broke it, reaching for her hand as he did so.

"I want you to know, Miss Woodruff, that although I did not elope with you as you planned, I still wish to help you."

She stared down at his large hand, holding her small one so firmly, and she fought back the feeling of warmth and comfort that was rising in her once more.

"That is very kind of you, Mr. Mallory, but you must not worry about me. I have already caused you quite enough trouble—and I truly did not mean any harm to Lady Luxley."

She moved her hand gently, thinking that she would extricate it from his clasp, but he retained it firmly.

"No, I am certain that you meant her no harm," he assured her. "I could see that immediately when the two of you met—and earlier I suspected as much, because you did not seem to me the kind of mean-spirited young woman who would do such a thing. I suppose that was why I was so angry with you. I felt as though I knew you, and then you disappointed me—or I thought that you did."

He continued to hold her hand and to stare out across the hills, so she left it there and gazed in the same direction.

Much later, he put his arm around her waist and pulled her closer to him. When she looked up at him, he bent and kissed her tenderly, and she wondered at such gentleness in so large a man— and one so experienced in love.

When that crossed her mind, she remembered Lady Luxley and sat bolt upright.

"What's wrong?" Mallory asked, startled by her abrupt movement.

She stood up and straightened her skirt, her cheeks darkening. "Lady Luxley!" she responded. "That's what's wrong! How could you treat her in such a manner, sir?"

Before he could say anything, she had hurried from the garden, quietly passing Lady Luxley who was reading in the library, and ran up the stairs to her chamber.

What a horror she was, she told herself, staring in the glass. She knew that Mr. Mallory and Lady Luxley loved one another, that Lady Luxley had run away from her husband and family in order to live with Mr. Mallory, and yet here she was—attempting to strike up a love affair of her own with the man that Lady Luxley had given up so much for. It was no wonder that Lady Luxley had cautioned her about her own reputation. She collapsed on her bed and wished herself on the other side of the world.

A little while later she heard Lady Luxley's voice at the door, but she closed her eyes and pretended to sleep. Still later she heard Mr. Mallory's voice, but again she did not answer. Soon enough, she knew, she would have to get up and dress for dinner. Even in circumstances as odd as these, she was confident that Lady Luxley would conduct daily life in as proper a manner as possible.

It would have been bad enough to be forced to sit down with the two of them, but now she would also be dining with her stepparents and the toad! Life, she thought, was not treating her kindly. She wished for all she was worth that she could feel about Mr. Mallory as she felt about Mr. Lanyon. There would be no problem then. Well, she amended, there would still be the problem of marriage, but she would not find herself wishing that she were marrying Mr. Mallory. How he would laugh if he suspected how she felt!

Chapter 9

When she could avoid it no longer, she put on her one extra gown and combed her hair. That was as much as she felt like doing to prepare herself for such a dreadful evening. She felt her forehead to see if she might have a fever, but her body did not cooperate. Sighing, she walked slowly down the stairs, putting each foot slowly on each step, as though she were a child playing games.

The others had already gathered in the drawing room and were waiting for her. Mr. Lanyon hurried to her side.

"Ah, Miss Woodruff, how charming you look tonight," he said, bowing low over her hand.

She snatched it away and turned toward Lady Luxley, who frowned at her and shook her head slightly.

"Remember, Vivian," she said in a low voice, "you must always be well-bred, even if you feel like picking up a poker and knocking someone down."

Vivian, grateful that she knew nothing of the

claret wine, nodded. She did not think there was much prospect of her behaving as well as Lady Luxley, but she could try.

In a moment, Mr. Lanyon apparently decided to make another attempt, and he closed in once more. This time, however, it was Mr. Mallory who interfered, frowning at Lanyon, who promptly turned and skipped back to his brother and sister-in-law. He desired no close contact with Mr. Mallory—and most especially not with a displeased Mr. Mallory.

Dinner was a nightmarish experience, and the only thing that saved Vivian was that she really did not participate. In fact, the conversation was carried almost entirely by Mr. Mallory and Lady Luxley, who appeared to feel no strain from the situation and talked amiably of art and politics, attempting unsuccessfully from time to time to draw in one of the others.

Vivian was dreading the moment when the ladies retired to the drawing room while the gentlemen sat over their port, but she was at least relieved to know that Lady Luxley was present. She had no intention of straying from that lady's side, no matter how much her stepmother wanted to speak with her alone. She was glad when the gentlemen joined them in very short order, the burden of a monologue having apparently grown too heavy for Mr. Mallory.

It was while they were having coffee that a footman opened the doors of the room and the butler entered, escorting a very frail, very elderly lady dressed in a black silk gown.

"Grandmother!" exclaimed Mallory, rising from his place to go and help her to a chair. "You should have let me know that you felt like coming down."

"I heard that we had guests, Anthony, and thought that I should greet them," she said in a gentle voice. She turned toward Lady Luxley whom she obviously knew, and extended a small wrinkled hand toward her. "Dear Diana, how are you?" she asked, smiling.

"Very well, indeed, Mrs. Mallory," Lady Luxley assured her. She drew Vivian from her chair and brought her close. "And this is Vivian Woodruff, a good friend of my Louisa, and one of the dearest young women in the world."

Vivian blushed at the compliment, but she managed a smile and a curtsy while Mrs. Mallory inspected her approvingly.

The others were introduced in turn and, as they were drinking their coffee, Lady Farrington looked at her with some annoyance. "I did not realize, Mr. Mallory, that your grandmother lived here with you."

"She does not," said Mr. Mallory agreeably. "Brexton Manor is her home, and I come from time to time to visit her."

Lady Farrington thought this over for a moment, then turned toward Lady Luxley. "And so you have been living here with Mrs. Mallory?" she inquired.

Lady Luxley nodded. "She has very kindly offered me a home with her for as long as I wish."

The matter of Lord Luxley hung heavy in the air, but no one mentioned that. Lady Farrington looked quite disappointed. The scandal that she had hoped to add fuel to at the next gathering of the *ton* appeared to have turned to vapor before her very eyes. Lady Luxley had not been living in a hideaway with her lover, but in a sedate manor with his grandmother. It did not, she thought regretfully, make a very lively story.

Vivian had been thinking about this herself, but she was, on the whole, pleased that Mr. Mallory had protected Lady Luxley's reputation by bringing her here. What she could not understand, however, was how the rumor had spread so widely without being corrected. And everyone knew that Lord Luxley had challenged Mr. Mallory to a duel and that Mallory had struck him in the shoulder, just as everyone knew that Lord Luxley had been searching for his wife for months.

Before Louisa had left Mrs. Chester's Seminary so suddenly, she had shown Vivian a miniature of Anthony Mallory and told her that it belonged to her mother. "She told me that he is dearer to her than anyone in the world except her children," Louisa confided. She had an older brother, Brent, who was mad for the military and had purchased a pair of colors. She and Louisa had memorized the face in the miniature, for Louisa had never met him either. Louisa had told Vivian that her father's jealousy had kept Mallory from ever being a guest in their home.

When Louisa had disappeared, she had left a note for Vivian and one for Mrs. Chester. Vivian had told no one about hers, and all that Louisa had said in it was that she was well and would be safe from any harm—and that she would write to her as soon as she could.

Vivian had puzzled long over that matter. Safe from what? Or from whom? She still did not know.

The whole matter, she thought, required explanation—except, of course, that she had no right to demand an explanation from anyone about anything. She sighed as she got ready for bed that evening. It was a puzzle that she would probably never solve—and as long as she did not have to marry Paul Lanyon, she could probably live without the solution.

Once in bed, sleep did not come readily. She kept remembering the stolen minutes in the garden, before she had reminded Mr. Mallory of his obligation to Lady Luxley. He had openly admitted to Vivian herself that he had had many lovers, but she hoped that Lady Luxley truly was his great love and that he would treat her accordingly.

And she tried very hard not to think about how she felt about Anthony Mallory herself. How pitiful she was that, knowing everything that she did about him, she could still find him appealing. She shuddered to think what that must reveal about her own nature.

When she went down for breakfast the next morning, she was horrified to discover that the only other person in the dining room was Paul Lanyon. She turned to leave immediately, but he had seen her and leapt to his feet, hurrying after her.

"Please don't leave on my account, Miss Woodruff," he pleaded. "If you will only give yourself an opportunity to become acquainted with me, I am certain that you will look upon me much more kindly."

He had caught up with her and showed signs of reaching out to take her arm. A sudden movement on her part brought him to his senses, however, and he snatched back his hand, remembering. He immediately glanced at her hands to see if she had anything in her possession that could be used against him. Seeing nothing, he relaxed and began restating his case.

She walked away from him, shaking her head, while he continued after her, still talking.

After she had taken several steps up the staircase, she paused and turned around sharply, catching him off-balance as he started up behind her. He scurried back to the safety of the floor as she waved a finger in his face.

"No, Mr. Lanyon! No, Mr. Lanyon! And once again I say no, Mr. Lanyon! I have no desire to speak with you, no desire to listen to you, no desire to see you—and most certainly I have no desire to marry you! Please, Mr. Lanyon, leave me in peace!"

Then she turned back and started up the steps once more, Mr. Lanyon climbing right behind her, as though she had not spoken.

"Mr. Lanyon! May I have a word with you, please?"

Mr. Lanyon blanched, for Anthony Mallory was beckoning to him from the foot of the stairway, and it was plain that the addition of the word *please* had been an afterthought. He walked slowly down the steps and, following Mallory's pointed finger, trudged toward the library. Vivian, on the other hand, went on her way rejoicing, deciding that she would have breakfast after all. For the moment, at least, she was free of Mr. Lanyon's attentions.

To her pleasure, Lady Luxley joined her there a few minutes later, looking very happy.

"I have just had a letter from Louisa," she confided, "and she will arrive tomorrow."

Vivian hugged her impulsively. It was difficult to know who was more excited about the arrival, Louisa's mother or her friend.

After a few minutes of conversation, however, Vivian ventured a comment that had been troubling her.

"It has been a very long time since you have seen Louisa," she said slowly. "I know how much she missed you after—after you left so suddenly. And now it has been several months since Louisa has been gone herself."

Lady Luxley nodded, her expression suddenly sad, and Vivian was sorry she had said anything.

"It has been a very long time, indeed," she agreed. "Far too long."

"Have you seen Brent?" she asked finally, hoping that might bring a more cheerful response.

"Yes, I have. It was Brent that removed Louisa from school for me."

Vivian looked at her in astonishment. "Then you know where Louisa has been all this time."

Lady Luxley nodded. "Oh, yes. I would have been quite wild with worry if I had not known. Brent took her to an old friend of mine—a friend I hadn't seen in some time—so that no one would suspect her whereabouts."

Vivian chewed her toast slowly, thinking this over. Who was Lady Luxley hiding Louisa from? It appeared to her that the only possibility was Lord Luxley, but she couldn't understand that. Still, she did not wish to pry any more than she already had, so she spread another piece of toast with marmalade and continued to think.

Lady Luxley smiled at her and patted her hand. "It's quite all right, Vivian. I don't mind your knowing—in fact, since you know Anthony Mallory, it is only fair to him that I tell you."

Vivian felt her stomach tighten, and she hoped

that she was not about to regret her tea and toast. She really did not feel strong enough to hear about a love affair involving Anthony Mallory.

"I left my husband, Vivian, because he was—he was not treating me well. Aside from occasionally striking me, which he had always done, he had begun locking me in my room for days at a time and forbidding the servants to let me out or to bring me food. They did feed me, of course," she said, smiling a little, "or I would have perished long ago."

Neither of them said anything for a minute or two, and then she continued. "He had always hidden his mistreatment of me from the children and he had always been fairly decent to them, so I had managed well enough. Finally, though, he took it too far and he hurt me quite badly, so I sent a letter to Anthony—who had been my dear friend long ago, for we grew up together. I knew that he would find a way to rescue me, and he did. Luxley told everyone that he challenged Anthony to a duel because he had run away with me, but the truth of it was that Anthony challenged him, even though I begged him not to. The only thing he did agree to was that he would not kill my husband."

She sighed. "I will never go back to live with Luxley, but it has been difficult to arrange. He cannot sell the property that I brought to the marriage, although he receives the income from it. Several months ago, one of the servants sent word to Anthony that Luxley was going to bring Louisa home from school and keep her there until I made satisfactory financial arrangements with him. That is when Brent took her away for me and hid her. I was afraid that Luxley had become so angry that he might mistreat her as he did me."

Vivian could think of nothing to say, but she rose and went to Lady Luxley, putting her arms around her and hugging her tightly. That lady had long been a lifeline for her, and it tore at her heart to think of what she had suffered.

"I am very glad that you had Mr. Mallory to depend upon, ma'am," she said, glad that she could say it with sincerity.

"And so am I, my dear. I don't know what I would have done without Anthony. He is the dearest friend I have ever had."

Vivian did not meet her eyes. "He is only a friend?" she said casually. "I had thought that—"

"People think what they wish to think. Anthony has always had a way with the ladies, and they simply numbered me among them." Lady Luxley dismissed what others thought with a wave of her hand, and she looked at Vivian with a twinkle in her eye. "However, it has seemed to me, my dear, that Anthony is greatly taken with you."

Vivian felt her cheeks growing warm, and once again she had trouble meeting Lady Luxley's gaze. "I believe he finds me amusing," she said in a low voice, "but that scarcely matters."

"Oh, I think it does matter, Vivian . . . and I think there is a great deal more to his feelings than that. Perhaps you should allow him a little time. I have noticed that you are rather short with him."

Vivian shrugged. "Perhaps. Just a bit, though."

"It's a lovely morning," her friend observed. "Why don't you take a stroll in the garden?"

Accordingly, Vivian took herself to the garden

once more, returning to the bench where she had sat with Mr. Mallory just yesterday.

Mr. Mallory, who had been lingering just outside the dining room entrance and listening with unabashed interest, strolled in. He patted Lady Luxley on the shoulder. "Thank you, dear girl. You did that very nicely," he whispered, walking toward the garden.

"You know that she will lead you a merry chase, Anthony," she called after him. "I look forward to seeing it."

He grinned at her and waved as he walked onto the terrace.

Chapter 10

"Good morning, Miss Woodruff," he said cheerfully, seating himself beside her once more.

"Good morning, Mr. Mallory," she responded, scooting over so that he had more than enough space.

"I needed to speak to you about a conversation I had this morning with Mr. Lanyon," he said, his voice serious, and she looked at him apprehensively. "It seems," he continued, "that he is quite determined to marry you."

Vivian shook her head. "He is quite determined to marry my money, but it will never happen."

"He tells me that he has the full support of Lord and Lady Farrington."

"Well, naturally he does! I told you that when we first met!" she retorted. "Lord Farrington obviously thinks that my father's fortune should belong entirely to his family."

Mallory shook his head sympathetically. "It is an ugly situation, Miss Woodruff. I can see how very unpleasant all of this must make your life."

Vivian was growing more and more aggravated. "Mr. Mallory, I can only think that you were not attending when I told you all of this. You act as though you have had a revelation."

"Well, in a manner of speaking, I have," he admitted. "And I have already shared it with Mr. Lanyon. I imagine that he has rushed to your stepparents to share it with them, so I imagine that we will see them any moment now."

"What are you talking about, sir?" she asked, puzzled. "What was your revelation?"

"That is exactly what I would like to know," said Lord Farrington, appearing on the terrace with his wife and brother. "My brother has been telling me some garbled nonsense that I find very difficult to believe."

Mallory acted as though Lord Farrington had not spoken, keeping his gaze firmly fixed on Vivian.

"My revelation, Miss Woodruff, is that I would like to elope," he said confidingly.

"Elope?" she repeated blankly. "What do you mean?"

"I had never thought you slow, my dear," he chided her. "After all, you had mentioned it yourself."

"I knew it!" exclaimed Lady Farrington. "I was certain that eloping was her idiotic idea!"

"And I thought it a charming notion at the time," continued Mallory, taking Vivian's hand, "but the more I have thought about it, the more it has taken possession of my imagination until I find I can think of very little else."

"You can think of very little except eloping?" she asked, watching his face closely. She strongly suspected that he was making a joke at her expense.

He nodded, holding her hand firmly. "With you," he added.

"I will never give my approval to your marriage!" said Lord Farrington, seeing a fortune disappear from beneath his very fingers.

"And did you realize, my dear," said Mallory, still looking only at Vivian, "that when you elope you have no need of parental consent?"

She nodded. "I believe that I had heard as much," she agreed. "That makes it all so convenient."

"I will have you taken up by a constable if you attempt to leave with my stepdaughter!" announced Lord Farrington firmly.

"And I have never yet killed my man in a duel," Mallory confided mournfully to Vivian, "only wounded them. It seems a sad void in my life."

Vivian nodded sympathetically and patted his arm with her free hand. "I should hate for you not to have that void filled, sir," she assured him.

Mr. Lanyon was tugging on his brother's sleeve and motioning toward the door, the mention of duels having had a disagreeable effect upon his digestion. It appeared that Lord Farrington might be feeling some of the same ill effects, for he was allowing himself to be pulled from the terrace.

"Don't worry, Lady Farrington," called Lady Luxley after the rapidly departing group. "I will be happy to chaperone the elopement."

Mallory pulled Vivian toward him and smiled down at her tenderly. "Are you still certain you wish to elope with me, miss—if I tell you that it will be no temporary marriage, but a very, very long one?"

She touched her hand to his cheek. "Are you certain that is what *you* want, sir?" she asked with a smile. "This seems most unlike you."

"I have been certain since I first saw you—it just took me a little while to recognize love when I saw it, having dealt all my life with only love affairs. Will you elope with me, knowing what you know of me?"

"Indeed, I will, sir, if you are brave enough to elope with me, knowing me as you do."

"You are right," he conceded. "I am the braver of the two of us. I was forewarned when I first saw the claret fly."

Laughing, he drew her close to him and kissed her tenderly. In the background Vivian could hear the crunching of gravel as Lord Farrington's chaise flew down the drive.

He had rescued her once more.

"I knew that you weren't a rogue," she assured him softly, her cheek against his chest.

"Ah, but I knew that you were a rebel, my dear, from the very moment I saw you," he responded, kissing her dark curls, "and I knew, too, that I had no chance against you."

Dance With Me

Lisa Noeli

Chapter 1

"Imagine that you are in a box, Miss Freely."

"What size is it?" she asked.

"An excellent question." Neville Dunsleigh smiled politely at his pupil. "A box big enough to hold you and a dancing partner."

"Oh," she said. "Well, then. I am in a box. A very big box. Now what do I do?"

"Please step, if you would, to each of its four corners."

After a moment's hesitation, she did so, but very slowly, counting in a loud voice. "One. Two. Three. Four. There! I did not trip on my dress this time."

Miss Freely stood stock-still, looking at him expectantly. Neville sighed inwardly. Teaching dance was not as easy as he had hoped.

Though Miss Freely was small and slight, she was clumsy. And she had a marked tendency to galumph, which was odd. He compared her mentally with another student of his, Mrs. Cuthbert, a very round and jolly woman, who was ever so light on her feet.

Dear Mrs. Cuthbert. Neville was quite fond of her, though she'd had only a few lessons. She was the sort of woman who kept up with all her cousins, wrote a thousand letters a year, and loved a good joke, especially if it was on herself, unlike Miss Freely, whose discreet cough brought him back to the present.

"Very good," he said automatically. "You have successfully completed a box step. You will be waltzing in no time."

"Oh!" she exclaimed, seeming pleased with herself. "Shall I do it again?"

He nodded patiently, watching her repeat the step, again counting loudly to four.

"I expect I shall be an excellent dancer in time." She looked at herself in the mirror—one of many propped against the walls of the small ballroom in the Freelys' cluttered town house. Paneled in expensive wood and its trim picked out in gold, the ballroom was empty save for gold-painted chairs lined up against the walls in readiness for a ball that would not take place until and unless Miss Freely actually learned to dance.

Thus far, her father had spent a small fortune on that goal. Apparently, there was nothing Mr. Freely would not do to please his only daughter, although Neville had been given to understand that this worthy fellow did not live with his family.

Miss Freely seemed pleased with her reflection and preened, patting her hair and turning this way and that. "All it takes is practice, of course. But I do prefer to dance by myself. It is much less confusing when only two feet are involved and both of them are mine."

Neville smiled. "The man must lead and the

woman must follow. When proper form is followed, the feet do not stumble."

Miss Freely giggled. "You make it sound as if feet could dance by themselves, Mr. Dunsleigh." She tried the box step again, picking up her skirts and swishing them about in a coy way.

Neville looked about for her chaperone, a Miss Eberhardt, who seemed to have magically disappeared. No doubt at Miss Freely's express instructions, he thought.

Still, he would not let her flirt with him. He wondered why she was doing so, since he was hardly the picture of masculine elegance at the moment.

He looked at himself in another mirror, noting that his dark hair was out of order and his shirt quite crumpled. Miss Quimp, his previous pupil, was given to dramatic behavior and missish fits, liking to act the lady without exactly being one. She had clung to him desperately throughout her lesson, as if he were a ruthless pirate about to fling her overboard into shark-infested seas.

Some women seemed to take dancing very seriously, no matter how nonchalant he tried to be. Though, in truth, he had decided to pass himself off as a dancing master for a very serious reason: he hoped to find a bride—one who loved the waltz as he did.

He used a pseudonym, of course. To ensure that his ruse would not be revealed in the few months he planned to keep it up, he had to take on all sorts of students—fortunately, he liked most of them. What woman did not love to dance, especially with an expert partner like himself? The boldest and youngest among them claimed there was nothing more thrilling than being whirled about for an hour or so, growing ever more breathless and rosy.

Even the worst dancers showed an enthusiasm that made their bumbling steps enjoyable—it seemed impossible not to have fun with them all. And Neville found treading through stately measures with respectable matrons equally enjoyable, due to their dignified good humor. Besides, they were likely to have a daughter or two, or some young female relation, not long from the schoolroom and eager to learn.

Neville smoothed the fine linen and ran a hand through his hair. Miss Freely, peevish and vain as she was, was not one of his favorites. He watched her awkward steps in silence. She might practice solo for as long as she wished, but sooner or later she would have to dance with another person. Namely, him.

"If I may, Miss Freely . . ." He caught her eye and she dropped her skirts. He extended a hand to one of hers and put his other hand upon her waist, bringing her closer to him.

She immediately stiffened into an awkward imitation of the waltz position he had demonstrated before. Neville found it difficult to keep a grip on her.

Bending backward, Miss Freely somehow managed to turn halfway round to observe herself in the mirror once more. He had an interesting view of the inside of her ear.

"Miss Freely," he said patiently. "You must not twist about like a snake. You will not be balanced properly."

She snapped her head back and looked him straight in the eye. "I am merely trying to achieve the correct posture, Mr. Dunsleigh. Have you not placed the mirror there for that purpose?"

"Yes. But you are not dancing with the mirror."

She narrowed her eyes, looking at him suspiciously. "What do you mean?"

"You are dancing with me. And therefore you must face me. In the waltz, you should look over my shoulder, just as if you were about to turn your head slightly and lift your eyes to mine."

"I was going to," she said crossly. "Do not forget, Mr. Dunsleigh, that you are no more than a servant. I don't take orders from the likes of you."

Neville bowed ever so slightly. "Of course not. I was giving advice, not orders. But the waltz is a sensual dance, Miss Freely. It must not be rushed. You should be pliable in my arms, and yielding. Sweet surrender—that is the effect we are after."

Her eyes grew suddenly round. "Sensual? Surrender? Mr. Dunsleigh, you are being most impertinent! I shall tell Mama of this at once!"

She flounced out, leaving Neville to stare after her with dismay. He was in for it now. Perhaps he should not have criticized her, but if she was piqued because he had not flirted with her—well, he had not wanted to flirt.

Miss Freely's mama was a judgmental busybody, whose cutting tongue was legendary—just one of many reasons that her darling daughter was now well into her third season with no prospective husband in sight. It did not help that her father, a wealthy brewer, lived elsewhere with an actress, as far as Neville knew.

He had never met the dissolute old man. The family solicitor paid for dance lessons in golden guineas, doubling Neville's fee per the instructions of Mr. Freeley.

Not that Neville needed the money. His father, the Earl of Abercorn, was nothing if not generous, though he was far away in Ireland. He had arranged for his London bankers to provide Neville with a handsome allowance, grateful that his eldest son did not gamble or squander it in other ways. Neville's bachelor apartments at Albany Court had been rented for a reasonable rate, and he spent only what he needed on clothes and so forth.

As he had told his dear papa, Neville had only one vice, if it could be called a vice: dancing. Certainly he was entitled to amuse himself for a season or two. Having dutifully swotted his way through a gentleman's education at Cambridge, Neville had learned everything he would need to know to manage his family's immense fortune and Irish estates when the time came.

If Miss Freely had the slightest notion of Neville's true identity, she would be happy to surrender to him on any terms. But he had not given her the slightest clue, playing the part of a hired dancing master to perfection.

She was not The One, in any case.

Certainly he would recognize his true love when they danced, Neville thought—he would not even need to know her name or anything else about her. He imagined the great moment: he would take her in his arms and she would move as lightly as a zephyr, eminently embraceable, held within the circle of his arms as if she—and only she—belonged there.

It would not be amiss, he thought, as he waited idly for the indignant Miss Freely to return, if his unknown beloved was beautiful, and witty, and charming as well. And biddable. He hoped to find a young woman with a talent for dance that equaled his own, and mold her into his perfect partner.

Neville was doing his best to find this paragon, attending every ball of the season. There seemed to be no end to such occasions. His own remarkable ability for dancing had been noted by no less a personage than Jack Chase, a handsome dancing master much in demand among the ladies of the *ton*.

The dashing Mr. Chase had instructed a multitude of blushing society misses in that exhilarating physical experience, the waltz—and some other exhilarating experiences. He had been happy to share his knowledge with Neville, who picked up the fine points of these popular pastimes in just a few nights at an establishment recommended by Jack. Neville had also learned much about dance from the older man, including how to teach it.

Neville hummed the melody of his favorite waltz under his breath. As far as finding his beloved, he had all the time in the world. Unlike Miss Freely, he was not expected to make an advantageous match. His father had told him that he might marry whom he pleased and when he pleased, and his gentle mother had murmured her assent.

Neville heard the echo of doors opening and closing within the house, as Miss Freely sought her mama. Very faintly, he heard the old dragon roar several rooms away.

He smiled to himself. If his employment here were to be terminated, he would be pleased as Punch.

Footsteps—the sharp strikes of workaday heels, followed by the lighter sound of soft dancing slippers—came closer. Old Mrs. Freely barged into the small ballroom, fixing Neville with a killing glare.

"Mr. Dunsleigh! My daughter says that you are talking of most unseemly things! Sensuality—and surrender!"

Miss Freely said nothing, smoothing her dress and looking down at the floor, the very picture of maidenly modesty.

Neville bowed. "I assure you, I have no designs upon your daughter's person." He noticed that the younger woman seemed a trifle put out by that statement. "I was attempting to instruct her in an effect—the appearance of yielding gracefully, if you will."

"There will be no yielding!" Mrs. Freely roared. "It was most unseemly of my daughter to send her chaperone from the room! Miss Eberhardt can consider herself sacked, if anyone can find her!"

"She is probably flirting with the footman, Mama," whispered Miss Freely.

Neville cast her a disapproving look. The chaperone was in no way to blame, but it would not do to contradict an old dragon. Miss Freely simply turned up her nose.

"Consider yourself sacked as well, Mr. Dunsleigh! And I shall not give you a character, you may be sure!" Mother and daughter turned as one, ready to exit the ballroom.

Neville merely bowed. "As you wish, Mrs. Freely."

"Simpsford, show him out!" the old lady called to the butler. "Throw him down the stairs if he resists!"

The imposing Simpsford, who had been waiting outside, walked stiffly into the room. He clasped his hands and stood there, waiting a minute until the sound of his mistress's footsteps died away.

"I shan't throw you out, Mr. Dunsleigh, never fear. But it is my duty to hescort you hither. Or is it hither? I cannot remember which is which."

"Do you know, neither do I," Neville said cheerfully.

The butler walked to the door and peered out to make sure the two women were gone. "I was wondering . . . you see, I am to go a-waltzing this Saturday night at Vauxhall, and I am not hexactly sure of the turn to promenade. It is a tricky business, and I should hate to tread upon a lydy's toes. Would you be so kind as to show me, sir? Themselves need never know." He nodded in the general direction of the vanished female Freelys.

"Of course, my good man," Neville said genially. He glided swiftly across the dance floor and demonstrated the turn, first to the right and then to the left. "It is simple enough. All it takes is practice."

The butler nodded. "Yet, the result is most himpressive, sir. I wish I had your savoir faire." He pronounced the French phrase in a way that left no doubt of his East End ancestry. Neville supposed that their mutual employer, Mr. Freely, probably came from similar stock and did not care.

He demonstrated a variation on the turn into promenade and the butler applauded. "Very nice! Very nice, indeed! Mr. Dunsleigh, you look like them gentlemen at Vauxhall! Why, you dance like a lord!"

Neville laughed outright as he collected his frock coat and hat. "Thank you very much, Simpsford. But I must work for my living, just like you." He could not let the man in on the ruse, of course. Servants were the worst gossips of all.

Looking into the mirror, the butler lumbered

through the steps he had been shown. "Naow, don't you worry about that Mrs. Freely. She is only a brewer's wife and her recommendation ain't worth a fig. The finest lydies in London would be lucky to 'ave you for a teacher."

"Thank you again, Simpsford." Neville bowed and waited.

The butler stopped in midstep. "For shame! Me frisking about and you ready to leave," he said. "Beggin' your pardon, sir."

Simpsford left off capering to show Neville out, keeping his countenance stern and his back very straight, should his mistress happen to see him.

Once the door had closed behind him, Neville heard the man's heavy feet practicing the turn to promenade and silently wished him well.

The spring day was fine and he was in no particular hurry. He wasted the better part of an hour looking into windows upon the Strand, taking particular interest in a display of pearl-handled pocket-knives before moving on to a display of porcelain vases and figurines that made him yawn, and from thence to the French bakery, whose window was filled with sticky delights. Two steps more brought him to the milliner's shop. He peered through the spotless glass, past the feathered and frilled hats that rested on mannequin heads, trying to see all the way inside.

Neville had no great interest in bonnets, but the women who patronized the place were particularly pretty; and Mademoiselle Olympia, the shop owner, was a talkative sort who made friends quickly with people from every walk of life.

He had made a most favorable impression upon the emotional little Frenchwoman when Jack Chase had first introduced them. She had let Neville place his card upon the cork-covered wall she kept for that purpose, where the bit of pasteboard jostled for attention among the other advertisements, including Jack's.

Through the window glass he spied a young woman looking at this very wall, though he could not be sure she was reading his card. He remembered leaving it at approximately eye level—well, at his eye level, but he was tall, and this pretty blonde was not.

Would she take it amiss if he were to enter and make some minor adjustment to the placement of his card? Would it seem absurdly obvious that he was trying to get her attention if he did so?

She turned to face him, as if she sensed his gaze upon her. Damn it all, she was astonishingly pretty. And graceful in all her little movements, which was something Neville tended to notice right away.

Her dress was the height of elegance, restrained in cut and color, but made of some luminous material that gave her a faintly theatrical air. Was she an actress? She seemed far too well-bred to be a member of that profession.

Her exquisite clothes fit her perfectly. A lace shawl draped her lovely shoulders, and lace mitts covered her slender hands. She wore a hat that let most of her silky hair show, adorned with a splendidly curling feather that seemed to beckon him.

He chided himself for that ridiculous thought but decided to go in and talk to Mademoiselle Olympia on some pretext.

The bell jangled discordantly as he pushed open

the door—he had not remembered it being so loud. Every woman in the shop turned to stare at him, including the blonde.

Mademoiselle Olympia bustled over, ringleted and beribboned as usual, and stood on her tiptoes to bestow a kiss upon each of his cheeks in the French style.

"*Bonjour, m'sieu!* It is extremely my pleasure to see you! And what brings our dashing dancing master to my 'umble shop?"

Neville suddenly felt a bit warm. The pretty blonde did not look directly at him, but there was no mistaking her subtle smile.

"Good afternoon, mademoiselle. I merely stopped in to say hello. See how business is going and all that." Business. Surely that was a sufficiently manly reason for him to enter this exclusively female domain, just in case the blonde was wondering.

"Very well, *merci*." She waved a plump little hand at a row of extravagantly decorated hats. "Here are my latest chapeaux, Monsieur Dunsleigh. Suitable for strolling upon the Pall Mall and guaranteed to attract the eye of every *gentilhomme*. What do you think?"

"They are indeed eye-catching, mademoiselle."

The petite shopkeeper picked up one and set it atop her ringlets, cocking the brim at a fetching angle. "I shall wear this one myself—I look three inches taller in it, *n'est-ce pas?*"

Neville smiled broadly. The Frenchwoman's vivacity and charm was irresistible, even though it was the pretty blonde who interested him at the moment.

But she had turned her back to him. He saw her draw a pin from her own hat and firmly stick it into a card of her own, which she placed in one of the few bare spots upon the cork-covered wall.

Mademoiselle Olympia picked up a slightly different version of the chapeau she was wearing and set it upon Neville's head, laughing merrily. *"Bien! Now we look like brother and sister!"*

Neville looked into the mirror, amused by the sight of himself in the overdecorated hat. Mademoiselle Olympia had a point. They both had dark hair and dark eyes and dimples, and wearing similar hats heightened the coincidental resemblance between them.

"I suppose we do, mademoiselle." He made her a deep bow and the hat fell off. He managed to catch it before it hit the floor. The other women in the shop laughed at the sight—but Neville noticed with dismay that the shop bell was ringing once more. The blonde was going out. He saw her outside the window for just a moment, proceeding on her way without a sideways glance.

He felt oddly disappointed.

Mademoiselle Olympia took off her hat and his, replacing both gently on the mannequin heads and fluffing up the feathers. "So! We have had our bit of fun, but you still have not told me why you are here."

"Ah—" Neville hesitated. "Have there been any inquiries concerning my card, mademoiselle?"

She shook her head. "Not since Mademoiselle Freely."

"Her mother has given me the sack."

Olympia looked at him a little more closely. "You do not seem heartbroken, *m'sieu.*"

Neville shrugged. "Miss Freely has two left feet and puts on airs. I found her quite disagreeable."

The shopkeeper sighed. "Yet her papa is rich. He lets her and her mama buy as many hats as they like." She pointed to a wide-brimmed horror, not quite finished but done up with bobbling ornaments that resembled fishing lures. "That is for his wife. No expense spared, he said."

"Of course," said Neville. "Mr. Freeley has a guilty conscience, my dear mademoiselle."

Mademoiselle Olympia's eyes opened wide. She loved a scandal. "Really? You must tell me why. Come, we shall take tea." She took him by the arm and steered him toward the back of the shop, waving an assistant over to take her place. "Giselle! See to the customers!"

"Oh—I cannot—I must be going," Neville pleaded.

"Non. I have ordered a cake from the French bakery. With *ganache* inside and *fraises des bois* on the top. I was expecting another friend, but he seems to have forgotten all about our rendezvous. You will do nicely in his stead, *m'sieu.*"

The customers in the store broke into titters once more and Neville knew the reason why. They simply assumed that Mademoiselle Olympia, thrifty like all her countrywomen, would certainly never waste a good cake—or a good man.

He let himself be dragged behind the curtain that separated the front of the shop from the back. He would ask Olympia about the blonde later—the little Frenchwoman would certainly tell him all she knew, if she found his story entertaining.

She waved him toward an armchair and took one for herself, pulling a small table already set with the cake and the tea things toward her.

"And now, *m'sieu* . . . in every detail . . . Miss Freely's last lesson. Begin!"

* * *

Several streets away, Miss Penelope Spencer congratulated herself for being brave enough to put up a card in Mademoiselle Olympia's shop. She had no choice—she had to earn her living somehow. Teaching deportment and elocution to social climbers seemed like something she could do without compromising her reputation.

Her clients would be young ladies, she reminded herself. Not social climbers.

Penelope wondered whether she should have asked the proprietress for permission. But Mademoiselle Olympia had seemed busy with that extraordinarily handsome man—whatever was he doing in a shop that sold ladies' hats, anyway?

She pushed the thought from her mind as she turned a corner and began the long walk home to a much more respectable street than the Strand, preoccupied with other matters—such as survival.

Surely teaching social graces was preferable to becoming a governess and living in a stifling attic room in someone else's house, with all the responsibility for raising the children and none of the respect.

Her benefactress, the elderly Mrs. Foxworthy, had agreed and volunteered the use of her best drawing room for lessons. Her house, a legacy from her dear, departed husband, was shabby but undeniably elegant. Fortunately for all concerned, it had been built squarely in the middle of what had once been one of London's most exclusive neighborhoods. Young ladies bent on self-improvement might not be impressed by the address, but their parents would be.

Mrs. Foxworthy had scarcely a penny to her name now that she was old, but she had a few loyal ser-

vants who had stayed on, willing to endure hard‐
ship for so kind a lady, so long as there was bread
on the table and a roof over all their heads.

Sometimes even that was difficult, when i‐
rained very hard. The bucket brigade rushed
about, catching drips in pots, emptying them ou‐
the windows, and quickly replacing them in strate‐
gic spots.

When Penelope was young, she and the servant‐
had made a game of it. Now that she was grown‐
she understood that it was not a game. But the house‐
hold needed more than ever to make ends meet
There was nothing she would not do to help Mrs
Foxworthy, just as that lady had helped the daugh‐
ter and granddaughter of her dearest friend, long
since dead.

She often said that Penelope resembled her‐
grandmother, Lady Spencer, the only daughter of‐
a duke. Mrs. Foxworthy still cherished an exquisite
miniature portrait of Lady Spencer, which Penelope
had seen. Her grandmother had also been a strik‐
ing blonde, with impossibly fair skin and eyes as‐
blue as a summer day.

Mrs. Foxworthy, a true gentlewoman, had re‐
mained a steadfast friend of the entire family, even‐
when the late Lady Spencer's daughter Caroline
eloped with an Italian dancing master. Penelope
had arrived seven months later and not prema‐
turely.

Penelope's mother, reviled throughout her short
life for this rash act, was soon found to have con‐
sumption. She had died only months after the birth
of her beloved little daughter; and Penelope's fa‐
ther, Giuseppe Pagnozzi, an instructor of opera
and stage performers, was taken soon after by the
dreaded disease.

On that unhappy day, the infant Penelope was brought from their modest apartment to a warren of backstage rooms and hidden there by Sally Webb, the wardrobe mistress at the Covent Garden Theatre. Months later, Mrs. Foxworthy finally discovered the whereabouts of the missing child. She had somehow persuaded the soft-hearted Sally, convinced that the baby would be left to perish in a foundling hospital, to give her up.

Brash to a fault, Sally refused to do so unless Penelope was brought to the theater to visit her often, which Mrs. Foxworthy had done over the years, ignoring the criticism of distant relatives who wanted nothing to do with the child of such misfortune in any case.

Penelope's cradle had been a stage trunk—a shocking fact. Her early upbringing within the very walls of a theater would be looked on as even more shocking, though it was no fault of hers, as Penelope's subsequent life with Mrs. Foxworthy had been a quiet one, except for visits backstage to see Sally Webb. Yet, Penelope loved the redheaded, loud-mouthed, coarse-grained Sally as dearly as she loved the gentle Mrs. Foxworthy.

By her eighteenth year, both women had agreed, sadly, that she could not be publicly associated with stage folk and suffer the vicious gossip they believed had shortened her mother's life. To that end, Penelope had shed the foreign-sounding name of Pagnozzi and had called herself Miss Spencer for the last two years.

She remembered nothing of her parents and did not want to spend a lifetime living down the scandal they had caused, since it had been forgotten. She hoped to start afresh. Each day was a new day, as Sally was always saying. The wardrobe mistress was fond of mottoes and embroidered the ones she liked best upon cushion covers during rehearsals, when she had the time.

It was Sally who provided Penelope's wardrobe, bringing exquisite dresses made for their leading ingenue from the theater when Penelope needed something pretty to wear. These Sally hid under her own ballooning smocks and brought back in again the same way. The stage door guard was a useless old sot, in her opinion, and not likely to notice a thing.

Though her two mamas, as Penelope fondly thought of them, had done the best they could, it was now necessary for her to earn a living. She and Mrs. Foxworthy had hit upon the scheme of teaching. Penelope had had cards printed up straightaway and added the number and address of a box in a general office several streets away to which discreet inquiries might be directed.

Surely her potential students—not to mention their desperate-to-be-respectable and frightfully rich parents—would not want the world to know that they were not quite of the quality. At least not until after said students were safely married to a title. Fortunately, they would have no way of knowing Penelope's history.

There was no one left living to remember it, save Mrs. Foxworthy, her remaining servants, and Sally. The wardrobe mistress had once sworn to keep her secret in the most melodramatic language imaginable, holding a prop dagger to her ample bosom and rolling her eyes like a stage tragedienne to make Penelope laugh.

She turned a final corner and hastened to Mrs. Foxworthy's house, noting with affection the threadbare but clean curtains that hung at its long windows and the well-scrubbed steps of white marble that led up to it.

They were keeping up appearances, as always—but if she could make a good match, there was hope for them all yet. Exactly how she might do that, Penelope did not know. She would have to be truthful about her background if it came to that. But what man would want a woman whose father had been an Italian dancing master, however blue the blood on her mother's side?

A week or so later . . .

Neville disentangled Miss Quimp from his shirt front. The day was rather warm and her unwelcome closeness was making him warmer still. Surely she must have noticed that he was sweating like a horse.

"Please do not cling, Miss Quimp."

"Do forgive me, Mr. Dunsleigh. I was not aware that I was . . . clinging to you." She gave him a melting look that reminded him very much of his dear mama's witless spaniel.

"Now. Back to the waltz."

"Yes," she said, very softly. "The dance of love itself, is it not? A mad rush into one another's arms, a giddy whirl through space, a fall into bliss unending at the crescendo—"

"I will settle for a basic box step, Miss Quimp. Again. One, two, three, and—Miss Quimp, are you crying?"

She whipped out a handkerchief and pretended to do just that, to Neville's annoyance. Still, her emotions might be real enough, even if the blasted woman could not summon up actual tears.

He did not know what to do next. They were in a public ballroom with other people about, but none came rushing to her aid.

Perhaps they had witnessed similar scenes before, Neville thought uneasily. He guided Miss Quimp to a spindly-legged chair and urged her to sit.

She obeyed, snuffling noisily into her hand-kerchief before blowing her nose with an unlady-like honk. "Thank you, my dear Mr. Dunsleigh. I was momentarily overcome. I promise you it will not happen again."

He nodded, patting her on the back. Poor little thing. He eyed the other ladies in the room but saw no more attractive prospects than Miss Quimp, who had at least had the intelligence to understand that she crossed a line that should not be crossed, and the decency to apologize for her outburst.

"Are you feeling better?"

She responded with another spaniel-eyed look at him and a hiccup.

"I think not, Miss Quimp. Perhaps we should bring today's lesson to a close."

She reached out a hand to his. "Oh, no! I must dance! I must!"

Neville found her hand was rather clammy. He returned it gently to her lap. "I do not understand your vehemence. What is it that you hope to learn from these lessons, Miss Quimp?"

"To free the deep heart of my desire, Mr. Dunsleigh," she answered in a throaty voice. "It throbs! It throbs!"

Oh dear. Was she in love with him then? How had that happened? He had not been in the least bit interested, had not given her the slightest encouragement—and had not noticed the approach of the pretty brunette who stood by him now.

"Oh, dry up, Quimpy," the brunette said cheerfully. "It's your big toe as what throbs, I shouldn't wonder. Did this tall gen'l'man step on it?"

Neville's dancing partner took refuge behind her handkerchief and ignored these impudent questions.

"Hallo," the brunette said, extending a none-too-clean hand to Neville. "You mustn't mind our Quimpy. Wants to be a lady, she does. Spends too much time reading them novels and fixing her hair in strange ways and learning to talk proper. But she grew up in my parish, sir. We was girls together."

"I see," said Neville, nonplussed.

"Has she fooled you so far?" She gave Miss Quimp a thump on the back. "Good for you, Quimpy!"

Miss Quimp drew herself up and threw a haughty look at her talkative friend. "Molly—you are interrupting Mr. Dunsleigh and myself. We were waltzing."

"Naow, you were sitting," said Molly. She winked at Neville. "But I have a little gift for you, Quimpy." She waved a lady's calling card about in midair, catching Neville's eye.

It was the very same one that the blonde had pinned to Mademoiselle Olympia's wall! The milliner had known nothing about the woman who put it there when Neville finally got around to asking her about it, and she had not minded his close inspection of it.

Private Lessons in Deportment and Elocution
Discretion Assured—For Ladies Only
Miss Penelope Spencer

* * *

The address listed was a box number, and Neville was none too familiar with the street, though he had a vague recollection that the neighborhood had once been good.

Obviously, Miss Spencer was a gentlewoman— her elegant posture and exceptionally fine clothes allowed for no other conclusion. But if she was forced to teach young ladies, she must have fallen into dire financial difficulties.

He had told no one of their odd encounter, except for Jack Chase, since Jack claimed to know every lady—and lady's maid—in London. But he had never heard of Miss Penelope Spencer.

Neville had gone to the address of the general office upon the card and wandered about the neighborhood, which had once been the height of fashion. The classic formal architecture of the houses and the charm of its picturesque streets made him feel a little sad that it had been forgotten.

Hoping that he might cross paths with Miss Spencer, Neville had parked himself upon a bench in the shade of a plane tree overhanging a quiet square. He'd watched the passers-by for an hour or more and debated writing her a letter and leaving it at the office, but having no pen, no paper, and no ink upon his person made this impossible.

When he returned to the general office, the clerk seemed distinctly unfriendly and not at all the sort of fellow who would lend such items for nothing. Neville had searched his pockets and found only a ha'penny.

Eventually, the surly fellow told Neville to be off and he complied, leaving the matter of contacting the intriguing Miss Spencer to another day.

He came back to the present moment with a start. The pretty brunette was waving Miss Spencer's card right under his nose in another attempt to rouse Miss Quimp.

"Where did you get that card, my gel?"

Molly looked at him a little suspiciously. "At the milliner's shop. Me mum works there part-time."

Miss Quimp seized the moment—and seized the card. "Hmph. Lessons in deportment? I don't need those, not if I'm taking dance lessons. And what is elocution? Is it scientific?"

"That would be electricity," Neville pointed out politely. "Elocution means the art of speaking."

Miss Quimp thought that over. "I might have to look into that." She slipped the card into her reticule, while her pretty friend wandered off in search of another of their acquaintances.

Neville made a show of looking at his watch. Their hour of instruction had concluded fifteen minutes ago, for which he breathed a silent prayer of thanks.

He had an idea. If Mademoiselle Olympia could be persuaded to give Miss Spencer a letter from him and say that Neville was her friend, it might serve as an introduction of sorts. The beautiful blonde was bound to come back and see if her card had been taken if she received no inquiries other than one from Miss Quimp.

Surely dear little Olympia would agree. He would have to stop by the wine merchants and buy her a bottle of some rare, frightfully expensive vintage, of course. But Miss Spencer was decidedly worth it.

Chapter 2

Two weeks later . . .

Neville could not quite believe that his haphazard plan had succeeded—or that he was now sitting across a table from Miss Spencer. True, the table was heaped so high with hat parts, trimmings, and feathers he could hardly see her, but she was smiling at him—she smiled like an angel in an Italian painting he had seen on the Grand Tour, he thought.

Though very young, she appeared to be a woman of uncommon intelligence, and she was even more beautiful than he had remembered. That Miss Penelope Spencer, who would easily show up the latest Incomparable of the *ton*, had no other prospects in life besides teaching ladylike behavior to the daughters of self-made men and merchants was simply preposterous—but he had to believe she was telling the truth.

She certainly believed that he was no more than

a dancing master, so it seemed only fair. No doubt she would not speak to him so freely if she knew who Neville really was.

Her voice was elegantly modulated and rather low; her manner, in every particular, that of a lady. It would be indiscreet to inquire as to exactly what unfortunate circumstances had driven her to earn a living— and Neville did not.

He hoped she would tell him someday, but in the meantime, he was quite content to just listen— and drink in her cool beauty while he was at it.

"Do you find, Mr. Dunsleigh, that the girls you teach are peevish and spoilt?"

He thought of Miss Freely. "Some of them, yes."

Miss Spencer sighed. "I find that nearly all of my students are. Except for Miss Quimp. She is somewhat older and so determined to be a lady it is almost comical. But I like her."

Neville merely nodded. It did not seem quite the right moment to own that he knew Miss Quimp as well. Certainly she did not clutch at Miss Spencer the way she did at him, so perhaps Miss Spencer had an easier time of it.

"Her mother owned a ship's chandlery and made a small fortune, which she left to Miss Quimp. She grew up amidst the swearing of sailors and the clamor of the docks, but you would not know it to hear her speak."

"Well, I suppose she would not go about saying 'furl the mizzenmast' and the like if she wanted people to think she was a lady," Neville pointed out.

Miss Spencer giggled. "I don't think one can furl a mast, Mr. Dunsleigh."

He thought about it. "You are right. Forgive me. I know nothing of nautical terms."

"Well, Miss Quimp does not use them. But she is a great one for flowery phrases. She reads too many romances, I think."

Neville nodded. "So you are teaching her elocution?"

"Yes. How did you know?"

"Ah—I simply guessed. It is on your card, of course."

"Which Mademoiselle Olympia was kind enough to let me replace when someone took it. I have had no end of inquiries since."

Neville smiled. "You are offering a valuable service, Miss Spencer. How else might the daughters of brewers and sons of merchants move up in the world without our aid?"

Miss Spencer let out a heartfelt sigh. "If only they would show up on time. They seem to think that they are doing me a very great favor by showing up at all."

"Time is a valuable thing, Miss Spencer. Particularly for those of us who charge by the hour." He ought to be struck by heavenly lightning for that blatant untruth, Neville thought, since he had never wanted for money in his life. But Miss Spencer had—and did now, from what he could gather.

"You must be firm," he added, moving the discussion to safer ground. "It would never do to keep a second pupil waiting because the first one dawdled."

She nodded. "Quite right. And I never allow it to happen. Though I have only been teaching a few weeks, it seems to me that these girls have never learned to respect anyone, not even their mamas. They think only of making the most ad-

vantageous match possible and talk incessantly of
it."

Penelope reflected upon the hypocrisy of her
last remark. Was not making an advantageous
match what she hoped to do herself?

She fiddled with a feather and did not quite
meet Mr. Dunsleigh's eyes. Truly, there was no other
way for a woman to escape from poverty, however
genteel it might be. But she had been much more
fortunate than many, thanks to the kind interven-
tion of Mrs. Foxworthy. Just the thought of the
grinding, low-down sort of poverty that swallowed
thousands of unfortunates made her shudder.

It occurred to her that she and Mr. Dunsleigh
were in the same boat, possessing the education,
tastes, even the manners and mores of the upper
classes—but not their income. They might live on
the edges of the polite world, but were forever ex-
cluded from it.

She became suddenly aware that he had shifted
his chair closer to her side of the table, as if he
found her utterly fascinating. Oh, dear. He was
rather too good-looking for her peace of mind,
and Mademoiselle Olympia was nowhere in sight.

The Frenchwoman had disappeared some minutes ago, not sitting down when they did and saying something under her breath about demitasse
and petits fours.

Then Penelope heard a sudden stream of words
in French coming from the next room. She was
grateful to see the curtain that separated the back
and the front of the shop move to one side.
Olympia appeared at last, holding a small parcel.
"*Zut!* The table is not cleared. Giselle! Where is
that girl? Excuse me for another little moment,

mes amis!" She added the parcel to the pile of stuff upon the table and went off again.

Neville looked at it carefully, noting the distinctive ribbon. The parcel was from the French bakery next door. Mademoiselle Olympia had taken an excessive amount of time to pick out a handful of petits fours, but perhaps she had done so in order to leave them alone, which was nice of her. He reminded himself to ask the wine merchant for another frightfully expensive bottle.

Olympia bustled back in, carrying an enormous basket over one arm. Into this she swept everything upon the table, with the exception of the bakery parcel, which she handed to Miss Spencer. "It is my way. Baskets hold everything. Like goes with like." She beamed at her guests, as if she thought of them in the same way.

He and Miss Spencer were indeed alike, Neville reflected. He was grateful that they had the experience of teaching in common—they would never want for something to talk about. However, just looking at her was a thrill beyond compare. He watched her carefully unwrap the parcel while Olympia went to get cups and saucers and silver, and was thrilled all over again.

What would it be like to hold her in his arms? He intended to find out as soon as possible. Miss Spencer might well be The One. If she could dance.

She had not mentioned that gentle accomplishment during their brief conversation. But surely a woman as graceful as she knew how. Why, even the way she untied the bakery ribbon revealed a fluidity of movement that told him much. She twined the ribbon absentmindedly around her little finger and gave him an uncommonly sweet smile.

Neville realized that he had been twined around her little finger at the same time. Miss Spencer was an enchantress, indeed. He leaned in, almost close enough to kiss her—but Mademoiselle Olympia came back in at that moment and broke the spell.

Neville sat back, as the Frenchwoman went back and forth, setting the table with a coffeepot and creamer, small porcelain cups and saucers, silver spoons and a sugarbowl, and tiny forks for the tiny cakes. She would not allow Miss Spencer to help her, but seemed pleased to be asked. Nothing more was said for a while, as the three turned their attention to the sweets and strong coffee she offered them.

Mademoiselle Olympia's eyes sparkled with happy mischief. Perhaps she might make a match—she had never seen two people more suited to each other than Miss Spencer and Mr. Dunsleigh.

She congratulated herself silently on arranging this successful tête-à-tête and getting the curious Giselle out of the way by closing the shop. These two seemed not to have noticed that no customers had come in for the entire afternoon, so fascinated were they by each other.

Bien sûr, Neville was every bit as charming as his dashing friend Jack, and Miss Spencer seemed to hang on Mr. Dunsleigh's every word, despite her well-mannered reserve.

As for Mr. Dunsleigh, he was clearly smitten.

Of course, the beautiful blonde was too much of a lady to reveal her feelings, but Olympia was French, and a woman—she could see right through Miss Spencer.

Olympia believed wholeheartedly in love, despite the complaints of her numerous customers on the subject. Men were fickle, men were unkind, men were interested only in themselves—the litany of woe went on and on.

Yet, if that were true, why did women desire them? Olympia supposed her customers could simply take the veil if they wished to avoid men, but none did. She reminded herself that there were no nunneries in England in any case.

There was a sudden lull in the discussion, and Mademoiselle Olympia spoke up. "More cake? More coffee?" The trick was to keep these two together as long as possible, contrive more occasions for them to meet, and seem to be doing nothing at all while she was at it.

"Ah—no. Thank you, mademoiselle," said Mr. Dunsleigh, who was not paying much attention to his hostess. He gazed instead at the blushing Miss Spencer, who twirled her fork in her empty demitasse cup.

Olympia realized what she was seeing: two people in love who didn't know it. Excellent. There was nothing more she could do. The rest was up to them.

Later in the week . . .

Was there anything more novel, more entertaining than the hubbub of a great city like London? If so, Neville did not know what that might be. The streets around Covent Garden through which he was walking were full of people, no less interesting for being generally disreputable, going about their business. Some, slightly better dressed than the rest of the crowd, simply strolled along, looking into shop windows and chatting.

A few women shouted out indecent suggestions, which Neville ignored. But he returned the smile of a pretty housemaid out upon some errand for a lady and winked at her. He was feeling his oats, he supposed. Ever since Miss Spencer had come into his life, he could not seem to think straight.

Their encounters thus far had been brief, but he counted them among the sweetest moments of his life. True, he had not been to her home, but his sense of delicacy allowed him to understand her difficult position which she had explained. The subject obviously pained her. Living alone as he did with an elderly guardian meant that she had little privacy. Hardly an ideal situation for billing and cooing.

No, he would have to get her out to Vauxhall for that—or to some public ballroom for the eagerly awaited moment when he might take her in his arms at last.

He was strolling down Panton Street, on his way to Garrard's jewelry shop to purchase a trinket for Miss Spencer. Nothing too fancy, nothing too fine—but certainly something that would gladden her heart.

Perhaps he might invite her to a performance of some kind. The theater was not far away, though he had no idea what might be on the bill.

Would she prefer comedy or tragedy? He pondered the matter as he walked. If the tragedy was heartfelt, with an ending to cry over, she might require comforting. He would be happy to oblige.

But a comedy might do just as well, in terms of its stimulating effects. Laughter and love went together remarkably well.

Neville decided that he could not go wrong no matter which he chose. Perhaps it would be best to

ask her before buying tickets in any case. A re
spectable young instructress might not enjoy th
raffish crowds that filled the London theater:
They were apt to fling vegetables and the like :
displeased with the play or the actors.

A shop window set at an angle from the stree
showed Neville his reflection from several pace
away. He noticed right away that he had a spring i
his step, and credited it to Miss Spencer. He swun;
his walking stick with a jaunty air. It was of ebony
with a mother-of-pearl handle, just the thing to se
off his plain but elegant attire.

Neville smiled inwardly at his vanity and tol
himself it was no great sin—and then he turnec
away and bumped into Jack Chase. There was :
short, stout old fellow by his side whom Neville di
not recognize, with a powdered and painted fe
male of indeterminate age hanging on to his arm

"Hallo, Neville! What the devil are you doing
here?" said Jack. "Allow me to introduce the distin
guished Mr. Freely. I believe you have made the ac
quaintance of his daughter and his lady-wife." Jacl
waved a hand at Mr. Freely's companion. "This i
not she. What is your name, my dear? I seem to
have forgotten it."

"Fanny," the woman said pertly. "Fanny Wilcox.'

"Miss Wilcox, this is my friend Neville Dunsleigh
He is also a dancing master."

She turned up her nose. "Hm. Another one:
London seems t'be crawlin' with 'em these days."

Jack gave her an injured look. "That is hardl
flattering, Miss Wilcox."

"Still, the woman's not wrong," boomed Mr
Freely.

Neville gave a start. He had forgotten the pres
ence of his former employer, distracted by the

sight of Miss Wilcox's ankles. She was bending down to scratch one and had hoisted her skirts to do so.

"Stop that," said Mr. Freely irritably.

She pouted. "But I have a flea."

"No need to let the whole world know it, is there?" The old fellow pried the painted creature from his arm and dug in his pocket for a few coins to send her on her way.

She tripped off down the street, waving goodbye. Mr. Freely pulled a handkerchief from another pocket and mopped his brow. "Good riddance."

Neville could only stare. He had heard the rumors about the old man's licentiousness but had not realized that a wealthy man would stoop so low. No wonder Mr. Freely lived apart from his family.

Perhaps Mrs. Freely had simply asked him to leave, in the interests of decency, and as a preventative against fleas. The thought was sobering.

Jack clapped Neville on the back in a hearty way. "I say, Neville, damned lucky to meet you on the street, and just when we were talking about you."

"What?" Neville hissed. He was relieved to see that Mr. Freely was eyeing the modest charms of a passing shopgirl and not paying the slightest attention to them. "How do you know him?"

"Mutual friend," Jack hissed back.

Mr. Freely sighed with unrequited lust and turned back to the dancing masters.

Jack's voice became suspiciously jolly. "Do you know, Mr. Freely hopes to hire you back. He will quadruple your fee. He means to marry his darling daughter off, and her new dancing master cannot manage the girl. Each lesson ends in tears and sulks."

Neville cast a wary glance at Mr. Freely. Should he mention that Miss Freely's last lesson with him had ended in the same way? Or that Mrs. Freely had thought him guilty of designs upon her daughter?

The worthy paterfamilias indulged himself in a scowl that looked just like Miss Freely's. "Name your fee, Dunsleigh."

"My apologies, sir—but I cannot. My schedule is entirely filled. In fact, I find that I must turn away pupils at the moment."

"I see. The ladies fancy you, eh?" Mr. Freely's scowl softened into something like a smile.

"Precisely."

"Oh, Dunsleigh's a devil with the ladies," Jack burst out. Neville glared as he tried to cover his gaffe. "Of course, dear old Dunny was the soul of propriety when it came to your daughter, Mr. Freely. You need have no fear on that score."

Mr. Freely scowled again. "There is no little Dunsleigh on the way, is there? Seems to me that the gel growed rather plump after you left, come to think of it."

"I did not leave—I was sacked," Neville said a little desperately. Why was it that explanations only made difficult situations worse? Yet, he forged on with another one. "I never touched your daughter, except to take her hand during the waltz."

"A wicked dance, that," Mr. Freely said thoughtfully. "I might try it meself. Well, I suppose it is the bonbons and cakes Edith eats that are to blame. Good-bye, gen'l'men."

The dancing masters bid the old fellow good-bye in reply and turned to walk away together.

"Jack! How could you be so stupid?"

"I just thought you might want the extra money,

Neville. Consider yourself lucky—no one ever offered me that much for an hour of waltzing, and I have much more experience than you do. Come. I shall treat you to lunch at the Lion's Tale and we can have a good laugh over filthy old Freely."

"Done."

They proceeded to the old inn, and emerged two hours later, rather the worse for an excellent meal and several pints of ale between them.

Neville had almost forgotten why he had come here today—to purchase a present for dear Miss Spencer. He had not told Jack one word about her, of course.

They said their good-byes and Neville went on alone. He noticed a display of necklaces and baubles sparkling in the window of a nearby jewelry shop and headed there straightaway. The place was not quite as fine as Garrard's, of course, but since he planned to buy something small, perhaps it would not matter.

He felt ashamed of his cheapness. Was Miss Spencer not worth whatever it might cost to win her? Certainly she was not the sort to be swayed by pretty trifles, but every woman loved them, just as every woman loved to dance.

It was all about romance—that was what women wanted. Miss Spencer was witty, beautiful, accomplished in her way, but she was no different from a great lady—or a dairymaid—in that respect.

And what ordinary men could not or did not provide in the way of romance, dancing masters did. Feeling smug, not to mention full of good ale, Neville silently congratulated himself on coming up with the best possible method to while away a season in London.

It would not last forever. He knew instinctively

that he had met The One. All that remained was to invite Miss Spencer to a dance or ball, and step out upon the floor together.

He remembered Miss Quimp's fevered words on the subject of the waltz. *It is the dance of love . . . a mad rush into one another's arms . . . a giddy whirl through space . . . a fall into bliss unending at the crescendo.* . . . He longed to experience the dance he knew so well with the woman he hardly knew at all.

A figure at some distance caught his eye—a young woman, whose face he could not see, moving toward the back of the Covent Garden Theatre. Her hair was golden; her dress, a luminous material that shone in the fading light of day. She reminded him of Miss Spencer, but it could not be she, of course.

Penelope lived many streets away and was not at all the sort of female who haunted the streets near the theaters. The young woman disappeared into the shadows, and he breathed a sigh of relief.

Neville began to retrace his steps, headed for Garrard's. He now planned to buy Miss Spencer something very nice, indeed. A discreet diamond bracelet, perhaps, that might be easily hidden under a sleeve or a glove from her beloved guardian, Mrs. Foxworthy. Neville would not want the good old lady to see such a gift and ask well-meaning questions.

There would be time enough for all that when the dancing was done, and he had asked the question that burned ever more hotly within his heart.

He practiced it in silence as he walked.

Miss Spencer. No. Too formal. *Beloved Penelope, brilliant star of my nights, bright angel of my mornings.* That was better. *Will you be mine . . . forever?* In his fantasy, she said yes immediately. He could not imag-

ne a different outcome. He would reveal his true
dentity, of course, at that moment, and there would
be the business of promising to provide for her hand-
omely, since she had no dowry or fortune.

Obtaining the consent of his parents would be a
mere formality. They were sure to be delighted
with Miss Spencer. She had said that her parents
were long dead. So that was that. He might as well
order wedding bands while he was at it, to save
ime.

He came to Garrard's and walked briskly inside.

Not far away, the object of his fond hopes sat in
a theater seat, quite alone, coughing a little from
the dust. Charwomen were moving through the
rows, sweeping vigorously in the hopes of finding
an earbob or other treasure amidst the detritus
eft behind by last night's crowd.

Penelope, who was waiting for Sally Webb,
looked idly about at the encircling tiers that rose
to the ceiling, and over the rows that descended to
the pit. She was the only person in the theater, besides the charwomen, of course.

She picked up the stub of an engraved ticket,
noting the title of the play, *CHAINS OF DESIRE*—a
thunderous melodrama that had packed the
house—and its author, listed only as "A Lady." It
occurred to her that she might write a play herself
someday—certainly she had seen any number of
them from the wings over the years, when Sally let
her scamper about.

The actors and actresses had made rather a pet
of Penelope in her girlhood, but she had always
been careful not to repeat their colorful language
or talk of their wild ways to Mrs. Foxworthy.

The most distinguished actor, spouting the greatest lines of the immortal Shakespeare, was quite apt to curse like the very devil once offstage. She had witnessed many a one yell for his ale or for a dresser to sew on a button or for the stage manager to fix a loose floorboard that had squeaked disrespectfully during his soliloquy. And the women were no better.

Ethereal though the actresses appeared on stage—the young ones, anyway—the illusion was created by thick layers of paint and powder. The delicate eyebrows and rosy cheeks of the leading ingenue were no more real than the scenery.

Sally must be busy with a fitting for that very lady, Penelope decided. There was nothing for her to do but wait and watch the stagehands.

Four brawny lads shoved set pieces across the stage, moving a Vauxhall backdrop done in pastel colors behind an enormous swan. The stage manager's boy lay curled up inside its papier-mâché feathers, sound asleep. No one saw fit to wake him, as theater children stayed up most of the night.

Another team of stagehands dragged in a Gothic dungeon in startling crimson and black. Its prop chains clanked and swayed as they positioned it behind the Vauxhall flat.

No doubt it belonged to the melodrama.

Penelope saw Sally step out in front of it, looking into the darkened theater for her. "Penny! Where are you, dearie? Ah—I see you! Come backstage then—tea is ready."

Penelope rose and scurried through the aisles, her footsteps echoing in the cavernous theater. She soon reached the stairs at the side of the stage, lifting her skirts to go up, mindful of the dirt the charwomen had missed. At least this dress was her

wn—a demure muslin sewn by Mrs. Foxworthy in
simple style—and not a purloined gown made
or the ingenue.

"Herself is gone," said Sally cheerfully. "You
ught to see her in her street clothes, Penny. A lit-
le draggletail, she is—she hardly looks the same."

Penelope smiled. "Stage magic. Women are
more beautiful, and men are taller."

"Hmph," Sally sniffed. "I 'ave no illusions about
hat."

She took the younger woman by the arm and
hey made their way through the maze of dressing
ooms and corridors backstage.

Sally opened the door of her domain and waved
Penelope inside. True enough, a Rockingham
eapot wrapped in a cozy was waiting, and there
was a selection of biscuits on a chipped plate.

"Tea is served, milady," Sally said grandly. "Did
ou know I once played a parlormaid in a pinch
nd spoke those very words to all of London?"

"I am sure the critics praised you to the skies,"
Penelope said with a smile.

"Not in the least. Sit down, miss. I had the prop
oy boil the water at the inn across the street and
ring the pot to me straightaway."

Penelope nodded. No one was more afraid of
ire than theater folk; and Sally had fled more
han one, saving what she could of the expensive
costumes and gewgaws before everything burned
o the ground.

Penelope pushed aside several half-sewn garments to make space on a small sofa and sat down,
surveying the platter. She chose a wholesome
wheaten biscuit, which she devoured, and fol-
owed it with one made almost entirely of sugar,
ust for balance.

Sally poured the tea—it was rather strong, judging by its dark color—and handed her a mug, "There you are. Now we are quite comfy. How goes your teaching, Penny? Are your students turning into fine young ladies?"

"Hardly," Penelope snorted. "They seem to be unable to walk and talk at the same time, let alone do it gracefully. I have them recite poetry and promenade with books on their heads, but all that is of little use when there is nothing *inside* their heads."

Sally laughed heartily. "Are you ready to give up? Was that what you wished to see me about?"

"I need some advice—about love."

Sally sipped her tea and raised her eyebrows simultaneously.

A neat trick, Penelope thought. She was not quite ready to name the man—Neville Dunsleigh—not that Sally would have the slightest idea who he was.

"Love, is it? Ay, that's a tricky business, Penny, and no mistake."

Penelope sighed. "I know. I suppose it happens to most people sooner or later—but does it always happen so fast?"

"My sweet! My innocent! My dowsabel!" cried Sally. "Has some blaggard trifled with you? Exactly *what* has happened so fast?"

"Nothing! I am pure! Oh dear. I don't know quite how to say this. I think I am going about it all wrong. But I have never been in love, Sally . . . it is all new to me . . ." Penelope trailed off and wrung her hands in her lap. She said no more.

Sally looked at her closely, as if the truth could be divined by a long, penetrating stare. "Are you in love? Are you sure?"

"I . . . I think so," Penelope stammered.

"Does Mrs. Foxworthy know?"

"Certainly not."

Sally set down her tea and rose to pace the room. This proved difficult, as costumes hung everywhere and the floor was littered with shoes. She sat down again.

"Who is he?"

"A dancing master."

"Oh my!" Sally's eyebrows rose all the way into her hair. She was silent for a long while.

"But he is quite a respectable man, Sally. And kind. And we are two of a kind. I cannot hope to make an advantageous match. Sooner or later I should be found out. He seems to understand what I must bear, and that is a very great relief to me."

"Have you told him *everything*?" Sally inquired after some thought.

"No . . . not everything. But he knows that I teach, and that I live with my guardian, a gentlewoman who raised me from birth . . . and that I have no money."

Sally shook her head. "You two will be as poor as church mice. It is not possible to live on love alone, Penny."

Penelope looked down to let a solitary tear roll down her cheek. "He has not asked me for my hand, but I think that he will. He is in love as well . . . I am sure of it. He just has not declared himself."

She did not notice that Sally was trying very hard not to smile. "What can I say to that, Penny? I have been in love more than once, and many a man has warmed my bed. But none of them stayed long."

"He will! He is different . . . he is a true gentleman, and I am sure he will keep any promises he makes to me!" Penelope burst out.

Sally patted Penny on the back in a vain attempt to soothe her, but the first tear was quickly joined by several others and noisy sobs.

P'raps it would be best to say nothing, the wardrobe mistress thought.

No. That would not do at all. Sally reminded herself that she had never been able to keep her mouth shut at the best of times. It was the redhead in her— even though her hair was now pure white. "Penny, stop that caterwauling. You can't think if you cry. Haven't I always told you that?"

This sage advice brought a trembling smile to Penelope's lips. "Yes."

"There, there." Sally patted her on the back again. "No man is worth making such a noise about."

"He is," Penelope said stubbornly.

"Is he now? And how long have you and the Prince of Promises been keeping company?"

"Less than a month."

Sally thought it over. "Then there is hope."

"You would not separate us, would you, Sally?" Penelope's voice was pleading, but the wardrobe mistress only laughed affectionately.

"No, ducks. And there's no need to play the tragic heroine. But you should not feel that you will lose him if you choose to go more slowly-like. A man in love is not easily put off."

She flung her arms around the older woman's neck and gave her a hug. "Thank you, Sally. You are a veritable fountain of wisdom!"

"A what?"

"Never mind. You have given me excellent advice. I would be a fool not to take it."

"I think you should know him better than you do and that is all."

Penelope nodded. It was hard to argue with that. Come to think of it, Neville Dunsleigh probably knew a good deal more about her than she knew about him. She had no stern papa to deliberate upon his prospects in life, and she did not have an anxious mama who would see to it that Penelope's true love kept a decent distance until her daughter was safely wed.

There was only Mrs. Foxworthy, who was now over eighty. Confessing a sudden passion for a man Penelope had only just met and never introduced to the old lady undoubtedly would be a tremendous shock to her fragile health. Penelope chided herself for her unthinking selfishness.

She would have to be careful not to be swept away, or venture into settings that inspired amorous feeling. Certainly she would not waltz with him—Neville had quite casually suggested going to a ball, but it might well prove her ultimate undoing.

"Drink your tea. Have another biscuit. And for your own sake, look before you leap."

The last was Sally's favorite motto, Penelope knew. She gulped down the strong brew without milk or sugar and nibbled on a biscuit, feeling better in seconds.

Chapter 3

Miss Spencer had disappeared—there was no other word for it. Neville was baffled. He had left letters at Mademoiselle Olympia's hat shop for Miss Spencer, which she had not answered; he had lingered at the places where they had spent those sweet, stolen moments; he had walked the streets of her neighborhood hoping to catch a glimpse of her; he had even placed discreet advertisements in several newspapers pleading with her to contact him.

There was no reply. Wondering and worrying about her led to sleepless nights. He knew he was not thinking straight, but there seemed to be nothing he could do about it.

At the moment, he was slumped upon a sofa in his Albany Court apartments, trying to imagine what he might do next.

He had a lesson with his plump pupil, the delightful Mrs. Cuthbert, in less than an hour, at her ballroom. He was as ready as he would ever be, he supposed. His valet had brushed his clothes, ironed his linen, shaved his face—and left when Neville swore at him for no good reason.

He was struggling to control his irritability still. He had no wish to take his temper out on Mrs. Cuthbert, who continued to astonish him by being the best dancer among his varied pupils, and always jolly to boot.

He had promised to bring her some diagrams of dance steps that she had requested—they must be somewhere in the miscellaneous papers and other things upon the low table in front of him, he thought. He rifled through them twice but in his distracted state could not find the diagrams.

Feeling crosser than ever, he swept the whole pile up and rose to stuff it all into the deepest pocket of his frock coat.

He could not disappoint Mrs. Cuthbert—he was quite fond of her. This matron, the mother of several grown children, even had some of the qualities he sought in The One, though Neville could not apply the term to her. She was old enough to be *his* mother, for one.

And Mrs. Cuthbert had long been happily married to a very rich man who had made a killing in real estate when London was a-growing. Mr. Cuthbert apparently liked his wife just as she was and made sure she knew it.

That thought made Neville pace the floor, his hands behind his back. Had *he* done enough to ensure that Miss Spencer knew of his deep feelings for her? Certainly he had listened to her attentively, paid a few compliments, and spent as much time with her as she would allow.

But perhaps he should have expressed his emotions sooner, and not been so damned polite. Perhaps she had not understood the strength of his hidden passion—he had done rather too good a job of hiding it, obviously.

Of course, he had not known her long or known her well, but did that matter? Now some other fellow who was better at talking than Neville had lured her away.

Neville had hesitated and he had stumbled—badly. What was true in dance was also true in life.

He vowed to redouble his efforts to find his lost love. He would give up teaching—well, he might keep the pupils he liked, just to stay in practice. He would give up sleeping—no, he had done that already. He would give up eating, except for beefsteak. Oh, he would give up anything but dancing if only Miss Spencer would come back to him.

Another thought struck him and he realized how silly he was being. Undoubtedly love and lack of sleep had completely addled his brain. He and Miss Spencer had a mutual acquaintance: Miss Quimp. He had only to ask her where he might find Penelope. He was sure she would oblige. Miss Quimp would ask for nothing in return save the privilege of clutching his shirt to her heart's content. It was a small price to pay.

He raked a hand through his well-groomed hair and ruined it. Blast! Perhaps Mrs. Cuthbert would not mind. She always seemed to see the best in people and superficial things like appearances did not interest her in the slightest.

Would it be wise to confide in her? She might be flattered. Mrs. Cuthbert had no one to advise, now that her own offspring had flown the nest. He would ask her what to do.

Neville put on his coat. Though the day was warm, it would seem disrespectful to arrive at her town house without it. What might be forgiven in a lord would not be in the case of a mere dancing master. He patted his pockets to make sure the papers she'd asked for were still there and went out the door.

Mrs. Cuthbert, who had been shopping, bustled into the ballroom of her town house. She was a trifle late, as usual, and followed by her long-nosed, bespectacled companion, as always. This odd person was charged with the responsibility of carrying the crewelwork bag that contained her mistress's dancing slippers, which she held with an air of disdain.

Dropping into a chair, Mrs. Cuthbert kicked off her street shoes and put on the slippers with her companion's assistance, being unable to bend forward with ease, chatting with Neville as she did so.

"Oh! I am quite out of breath, Mr. Dunsleigh! We must start slowly today."

He bowed. "Of course, Mrs. Cuthbert." The long-nosed companion slunk away to some dark corner. Mrs. Cuthbert had told him that her companion disapproved of dancing.

"I have engaged a pianist just for us," she said brightly. "My husband says that an orchestra is an extravagance, even if it is a little one. So we must make do."

"Indeed," said Neville. Last time there had been a violinist, scraping away mercilessly at his instrument until they told him to stop and hummed the music themselves; and the time before that, there had been a Spanish guitarist who was not at all sure what a waltz was. But Señor Gutierrez had played stirring dances of his native land, and Neville and Mrs. Cuthbert had invented new steps to go with them.

Neville smiled automatically and offered his hand to steady her rise. He took her into his arms just as automatically, and they moved about the floor to the dogged melody that was being pounded out upon a pianoforte at the end of the room. Unfortunately, the musician was more determined than artistic and repeated the melody over and over.

"At least it is easy to follow," Mrs. Cuthbert giggled. *"Dum-dum-dum. Dum-dum-dum. Dum-dum-dum-dee."*

The monotonous notes echoed in Neville's sleepless brain. "Yes. It is." He noted in a daze that Mrs. Cuthbert moved with enviable grace, no matter how bad the music or how little attention he was paying.

They danced still more slowly about the floor. The ballroom, though spacious, seemed quite warm to Neville. He felt, not surprisingly, overwhelmed by a compelling drowsiness. His chin dropped to his chest, but he jerked his head up, peering blearily at Mrs. Cuthbert.

"Are you unwell, Mr. Dunsleigh?" she asked anxiously.

"Yes. I mean, no," he forced himself to say. "I am quite well. And how are you, my dear Mrs. Cuthbert?"

Dum-dum-dum. Dum-dum-dum. Dum-dum-dum-dee. He did not hear her answer but swayed helplessly against her. The room was spinning.

"Mr. Dunsleigh!"

He let go of her hands, collapsed upon her stately

bosom, and then slowly slid to the floor. Everything went black.

"He has fainted! Someone—come quickly!"

Neville awoke in an unfamiliar room, the mishap at the Cuthberts' ballroom coming back to him little by little. He had been dizzy. He must have fainted. Mrs. Cuthbert had had him brought to another room within her house.

He struggled to sit up. Was he alone? Yes, except for a huge tabby cat that looked at him solemnly through glowing eyes. No doubt it had entered the room on silent paws and been forgotten about. The moonlight and shadows—and most particularly, the watching cat—unnerved him.

Yet, he felt refreshed. He yawned and stretched.

He seemed to be in a library. Mahogany shelves, neatly partitioned, rose to the ceiling. There was a bar of light—warm, golden, welcoming light—under the massive double doors to the room.

Neville looked down to make sure he was fully dressed. He was, though there was no telling where his shoes or coat were. He padded to the doors in stockinged feet and tried to open them. They were locked, and the key was outside.

What the devil was going on? He pounded on the door and, after a minute, heard light footsteps come his way.

Mrs. Cuthbert burst in. "My dear Mr. Dunsleigh! Are you recovered? I thought you might wander when you woke and so I locked you in—I do apologize. Henry, come quickly!" A manservant followed her into the library. "Mr. Dunsleigh is feeling better and we must get him home."

She put her hands on her hips and gave him a sly look. Neville scrubbed a hand over his face to wake himself up and wondered what the look was for.

Mrs. Cuthbert was the kindest and most even tempered of women, not given to strange behavior, as far as Neville knew. He stifled another yawn and inquired after his shoes.

"Oh, yes. They are in there." She indicated the basket that Henry had over his arm. "Along with your watch and a few other things. I found the dance diagrams and I am keeping those. But I feel obliged to return some papers that make it clear you are not Mr. Dunsleigh at all, though your first name is Neville."

He swallowed hard. Damn and blast. He had given himself away. The huge tabby cat shot past him to freedom as Mrs. Cuthbert laughed merrily.

"Yes! The cat is out of the bag at last! You are an impostor—though it seems that you are also the eldest son of the Earl of Abercorn. And do you know, my second cousin has lived long in Ireland. She is a bosom friend of the countess, your mother. But I have never met any of them, of course. Now tell me where you learned to dance so well, my lord!"

Neville drew a deep breath but did not reply. He held out a hand for the basket and fished in it for the papers, gathered in such haste, which had betrayed him. There was a bank draft upon the Abercorn account in his real name and a letter from the earl to his solicitor explaining the terms and conditions of Neville's stay in London. The old man had made particular mention of his son's love of dancing.

There was a drawing of two hearts, linked, bear-

ng his initials and Penelope's. He crumpled this
up straightaway rather than explain it.

There was also an unframed miniature of himself and his fond mother done a few years ago,
clearly labeled with both their names. He could
not argue his way out of that.

"My dear Mrs. Cuthbert," he began. "I thought to
amuse myself. That other people would be affected
by my harmless deception never entered my mind."

She laughed again. "Think nothing of it! I find
it most amusing!"

"Penelope will not." Neville sighed gloomily. He
handed her the basket, which she passed along to
Henry, keeping her hand affectionately on Neville's
arm.

Mrs. Cuthbert's eyes lit up. "Is she the P.S. in the
heart? Are you in love, dear boy? Come to the
drawing room and tell me all about it. Henry, tell
Cook to prepare a midnight supper. There should
be a cold lobster or two unless the cat got at it."
She gave Neville's arm a maternal pat. "Just us two.
Mr. Cuthbert has been asleep for hours and he is
not interested in *affaires de coeur*, anyway. But I am.
Oh, Neville—may I call you Neville? I feel as if you
are a new relation! This is most exciting!"

The sky was lighter in the east when he finally
finished telling the whole story. Mrs. Cuthbert had
quizzed him thoroughly on every detail and repeated the names to make sure she had everyone
straight.

She sighed over the ill-starred romance and
wept a little at the thought of lovers parting for no
apparent reason.

"There is only one thing to do, Neville. You must find Miss Spencer . . . and you must tell her the truth. Promise me that you will do so."

"I promise. But she might not trust me."

"You did lie to her, but you meant no harm and no real harm was done. And it is clear that you adore her. But when you find her, Neville, you must remember one thing."

"And what is that, Mrs. Cuthbert?"

She settled herself deep into her armchair before replying. "It seems to me that you are rushing things. Did you not tell me that a dancer should savor each step and not seem to scramble over the floor in a dreadful hurry to arrive at nowhere?"

He nodded. "My exact words."

"Well, then. Have patience. Penelope will need time to get to know you, and to fully understand her feelings. You are young, but she is younger. A long engagement is best in such circumstances. You must learn who you are before you marry, my boy."

"May I ask you a question, Mrs. Cuthbert?"

"Of course."

"How old were you when you married?"

"Nineteen."

"And how long had you been engaged?"

"Two weeks. I was impetuous. And Mr. Cuthbert was a fiery young man of twenty-five, determined to make his mark upon the world with me by his side. Oh, but he was handsome—and here he is!"

Neville heard a shuffling sound of old carpet slippers behind him and turned to see Mr. Cuthbert. He was no longer fiery but stooped and gray. Still a warm affection for his wife shone in his eyes. "Good morning, my dear. Shall we breakfast in bed? You can tell me everything."

"Yes, love. Good night, Neville—I mean good morning, I suppose! We will talk again later."

The long-married couple left the room arm in arm, and Neville sat there thinking for at least an hour more.

Chapter 4

Neville told the story again, although not in such exhausting detail, to Miss Quimp. She seemed flabbergasted to learn that she had been dancing with a real lord and gazed at him in wonder as if he were something other than a mortal man. She was deeply touched by the story of the star-crossed lovers, though Neville did not refer to himself and Penelope in those words. But Miss Quimp agreed to give his letter to Miss Spencer.

In it he had explained everything, humbly begged her forgiveness, taken all blame for misleading her as he had, folded it, addressed it, sealed it with wax, and kissed her name when the ink was dry. But Miss Quimp did not need to know those details either. Her spaniel eyes were suspiciously wet as it was. Still, the idea of playing Cupid and carrying letters seemed to appeal to her romantic soul.

"I should be honored to bear a missive in return, Lord Abercorn," she said. "But I cannot give away her whereabouts without her permission.

She is kind, and beautiful—and she has taught me so much!"

"I understand, Miss Quimp," Neville said gently. "I will wait however long it may take for her reply."

Miss Quimp breathed deeply, as if passion were in the very air of the perfectly ordinary square in which they sat on a perfectly ordinary bench made of wrought iron. A flock of starlings settled on the grass and squawked noisily.

"That reminds me. I read a poem once," she said softly, "in which a lady was imprisoned in a tower. Her faithful lover sent her a letter everyday, delivered by nightingales."

"Surely Miss Spencer is not imprisoned," Neville said. Would Miss Quimp never leave? It was of utmost importance that his letter be delivered as soon as possible. He quelled his panic and reminded himself not to rush.

"Of course not. But she guards her privacy." Miss Quimp gathered up little things she had dropped, patting at her disheveled hair and putting her dress in order. She seemed to be a person who went to pieces quite easily, Neville thought. He hoped the letter would get to its destination unharmed and unopened.

At the moment, she was his only hope. Mademoiselle Olympia had shaken her head sorrowfully when Neville had inquired there earlier in the day, murmuring something about *chagrin d'amour.* He believed it meant "the pain of love," a miserable experience that sounded much nicer in French.

"Good day, Lord Abercorn."

He escorted her from the square and to a hackney coach that he had paid to wait there until Miss

Quimp's departure. Of course, he could simply bribe the man holding the reins of the broken-down nag that pulled it to return. It would be an easy way to learn the secret of Miss Spencer's address—but that seemed not in keeping with his vow to Mrs. Cuthbert to tell the truth from now on.

He wandered down the street to the Strand, indulging in his customary pastimes of window shopping and people watching. It was as good a cure as any for the loneliness in his heart. Fueled by a meat pasty or two along the way, Neville found himself an hour or so later at the corner of Cockspur Street and followed it to Haymarket, thinking idly of the theaters there. It was now late afternoon and there was time to buy a ticket for a play.

He could even have a proper meal at the Lion's Tale, once the ticket was safely in his pocket. It suddenly occurred to him that he had not been back to Garrard's since ordering Miss Spencer's pretty little diamond bracelet and a double set of wedding rings. Had he really been so sure of himself—or her? The thought saddened him. That day seemed long past, but in truth it had not been long ago.

He might pick up the bracelet at least—he would tell the jeweler to keep the rings for a little while longer.

He was replete with good food—quite stuffed, in fact. Neville had been too hungry to buy his ticket before going to the Lion's Tale. He left, picking his teeth with an ivory toothpick—there was no one to care if he did.

He studied the bills slapped up on the sides of the theater and every other vertical surface. *A MAN AND A MAID. A Rollicking Farce!* Alas, love was not an amusing subject at the moment. He moved along to the next. *THE CANNON'S ROAR. A Military Drama with Full Orchestra!* He feared for his hearing. *MISS DIDDLE'S DILEMMA. A Genteel Comedy for All!* Much ado over the teacups, he imagined.

No, he might as well return home. He was not far from Albany Court and a postprandial stroll would do him good.

A woman in a tattered dress came forth from out of the shadows and made him a lewd proposition in a sad little voice. Neville shook his head, feeling nothing but pity for the poor creature. She and her kind had worked the mean streets around these theaters for generations. He walked on, lost in thought and not paying attention to where he was going—in the opposite direction from Albany Court and Piccadilly Street.

By twists and turns, he found himself at the Covent Garden Theatre once more. The crowd had gone in for the first act, and he could hear them applaud noisily, though it was only for the orchestra, which was warming up.

As he had once before, Neville saw a woman moving swiftly by—and he saw her face this time. It was Miss Spencer! He was sure of it. She took one look at him and ran into the theater by the stage door.

The beefy guard posted there let her through—but he stopped Neville.

"Let me pass! I know that lady!"

"Do I have to break yer neck and throw ye in the

gutter with the rest of the dead cats? Be off!" He pushed Neville hard and sent him sprawling upon the cobblestones, then went inside, slamming the door behind him.

Neville got up slowly, rubbing his leg. Very well. He would have to buy a ticket, no matter what the play. He hobbled to the ticket seller's booth and handed over the required sum to the gnome behind the glass. There were but two seats left, the gnome explained, in the lower rows. Neville handed over more money and bought both.

He limped down the aisle, led by an usher who kicked the legs of those who dared to let them sprawl in the aisle.

These patrons of the arts responded by shaking their fists and cursing. Neville clambered over them and took his place. He could see well into the wings, a disadvantage to devoted theater-goers, perhaps—but it was precisely the position he needed to be in to catch a glimpse of Miss Spencer backstage, if that was where she had gone.

So she did have some connection to the theater— there was no other reason for her to be here, unless she was giving elocution lessons to country-bred actresses. He suddenly remembered his first impression of Miss Spencer in Mademoiselle Olympia's shop, when he had wondered if she was an actress.

With a crash of cymbals that nearly made Neville jump out of his skin, the performance began.

It seemed to be a love story, complete with a sighing swain and his bosomy lovey-dove and scheming relatives who wanted the hero and heroine to marry someone else and not each other.

The boisterous audience seemed to agree, especially when the cast burst into song at odd moments.

Actors came and went in a confusing way, and the louts in the low rows began to lose interest. A decrepit cabbage was hurled upon the stage, to wild applause. A limp head of celery followed.

A cheeky little miss scampered upon the stage, piped her lines, and delighted the louts by throwing the celery back.

Neville watched intently, but he was not looking at the play. Ah! There she was—backstage, just as he thought. Penelope's golden hair was unmistakable. A buxom woman stood next to her, helping the actors with quick costume changes or shooing them away into unseen dressing rooms.

There was nothing for it. She would disappear in the crowd when the play was over. He had to get to her. Now.

Neville got up, ignoring the loud complaints of those seated behind him. He made his way slowly past those seated in his row, unable to move quickly, stiff from his tumble upon the cobblestones.

He kept his head down, hoping Penelope would not see him beyond the footlights. There was so much happening onstage, it was quite possible that she would not.

One more seat and he would reach the aisle. But the sleeping man in it was massively built and blocked his way. Neville wrinkled his nose at the smell of sour ale the man exuded with each breath.

He extended a long leg over the sleeper and winced. A stabbing pain in his back forced Neville to sit down heavily in the drunken man's lap.

"Harh?" The man opened bloodshot eyes. "Wha? Get the hell off!"

Neville couldn't move, but the drunk could. He picked Neville up and flung him into the aisle.

"As if the whores ain't bad enough!" he growled.

"Wot is the world comin' to, hey?" The drunk settled back into his seat, leaving Neville to rise with great difficulty and stagger down the aisle. The side stairs to the stage—he had to reach them. He could still see Penelope and he was still sure she had not seen him.

A stagehand rose from the pit to stop him at the foot of the stairs—a slight lad, Neville noticed. He pushed him back into the pit and went up the stairs, reaching the wings in a few seconds.

Penelope gaped at him. "Oh!"

The buxom woman standing beside her grabbed the scissors that hung from a ribbon around her neck and waved them at Neville. "Back! Back, I say!"

Neville wanted to laugh. It was that, or cry.

"Oh, Neville!" Penelope exclaimed softly.

The buxom woman let go of the scissors. "Is this the man you love, Penny? He can hardly walk!"

"What of it?" Neville said. "I am here. I have found you, Penelope . . . did you get my letter?"

"Yes," she breathed. "I understand."

The stage manager hurried over to see what the commotion was all about. "Now see 'ere, young man. Ye can't just go a-barging into a first-class production featurin' seventeen original songs. We 'ave a full 'ouse tonight, too! I oughter have ye thrown out, but our lucky Penny seems to know ye!" He looked to the right and left. "Hang it, the dance number is about to begin!"

A horde of female performers clad in pinkish stockings and swathed in matching tulle rushed into the wings and awaited their cue to go on. One of the bigger ones added insult to injury by stepping very heavily on Neville's left foot.

"Are you in this scene?" she asked in a venomous whisper.

"I don't think so," Neville said, feeling slightly woozy.

"Oh, Neville! Your toes!"

He put his arms around Penelope, not caring who saw them embrace. "It matters not, my sweet. Just say that you love me, even if I lied. I promise never to do it again."

"I lied, too," she whispered.

"You did?" Neville's voice was loud in the sudden silence.

"Hoi! You there! Shut yer gob!" whispered the dancer who had stepped on his foot. She moved closer to the stage with the others, but they stayed just inside the wings.

Neville and Penelope retreated into the shadows. "I explained everything in my reply," she said sadly. "Miss Quimp has it."

"Then I will read it tomorrow. In the meantime—"

He broke off to see the dancers take their cue from the stage manager and pirouette onstage two by two as the orchestra began to play . . . a waltz.

"Yes, Neville? What shall we do in the meantime?"

"Dance with me."

Then and there, in the alternation of deep shadows and brilliant beams of light that pierced the backdrop, they waltzed together for the first time. Neville silently vowed it would not be the last.

He limped. She stumbled. But they were perfect together—he knew it in his soul. All they needed was practice.

He made her stop and brought her more closely

within the circle of his arms. He kissed her. And he kissed her again.

The waltz ended and the dancers scampered off. Neither Neville nor Penelope noticed when the backdrop rose and the audience saw them kiss. For a few seconds, the theater-goers seemed to assume that it was part of the play, which had made no sense anyway.

Neville turned slightly and caught a glimpse of the packed house. He kissed Penelope again, quite thoroughly. The crowd went wild.

They jumped apart, made a hasty bow, and exited left.

Chapter 5

He had to marry Penelope at once. Neville was delighted that she had agreed—with the collective blessing of Mrs. Foxworthy, Mrs. Cuthbert, Sally Webb, Mademoiselle Olympia, and Miss Quimp.

Though Neville certainly understood Mrs. Cuthbert's wise advice on the dangers of rushing, it was not possible to do otherwise. He had given an innocent young woman a passionate kiss—several passionate kisses, in fact—in front of a thousand people.

The memory of their applause still made him feel warm all over. Now he understood why actors loved the stage. The attention was delicious. Of course, he would never tread the boards himself.

They were to be wed in the Church of St. Paul that overlooked the Covent Garden piazza. It was the church of theater folk—they had been made honorary members of the Covent Garden company by its director, though Neville had not reported that shocking fact to his conservative parents.

Once they were married, they would go to Ireland for their honeymoon. Neville had planned it all to the last detail. Nothing could go wrong.

His parents had invited them to take over a wing of their magnificent house, which came with a separate staff of nine servants and a very fine cook, but Neville wrote that he and Penelope preferred to travel incognito, and stay at inns and rose-covered cottages featuring decorative sheep.

Penelope had put her foot down firmly upon that romantic notion and insisted on the magnificent house, the servants, and all the comforts she didn't have at home.

More than anything else, she wanted to wake up in a bed of baronial splendor, beside the man she loved, under a roof that didn't leak.

Neville thought that could be arranged. But he kicked at the idea of staying with his parents indefinitely. They compromised on hiring the best architect in London to design a house that would be all their own. It would have a ballroom, of course.

He had advised Penelope on what to bring until he realized that Sally Webb was emptying the theater closets to provide her trousseau. He returned all the gowns and multiple pairs of shoes to her with the assistance of Miss Quimp, and bought a new wardrobe.

Neville and Penelope became man and wife in a simple ceremony, with a steady rain drumming upon the roof of the church. Sally said rain was lucky for a wedding, and no one wanted to argue with Sally.

Penelope kept up a correspondence with all her beloved friends, and Neville's as well, in the months that followed. Mrs. Foxworthy, contentedly at home, as she was too frail to travel, always answered promptly and filled her in on everyone's doings in no particular order.

Mademoiselle Olympia stopped by often to play whist. Her gorgeous hats were all the crack (Mrs. Foxworthy put slang like this in careful quotes) among the *ton*.

Jack Chase was now teaching Miss Quimp, a fact that Neville confirmed. He had met his former colleague at the Lion's Tale on one of his trips to England and listened sympathetically to Jack's complaints about clutching.

Mrs. Cuthbert had become proficient in the waltz and planned to open an Academy of Dance. There was even more joyous news from that quarter: the first Cuthbert grandchild was expected, and the production of tiny knitted garments had begun immediately.

Penelope's constant financial help was a blessing, indeed. The house badly needed repair and Mrs. Foxworthy saw no reason to refuse. It gladdened her heart that Penelope provided so handsomely for her in her old age, as she had no children of her own.

Sally Webb, another frequent visitor, provided Mrs. Foxworthy with pillows to cushion her arthritic knee. The wardrobe mistress seemed to have an endless supply, and all were embroidered with uplifting mottoes, Mrs. Foxworthy noted.

And Miss Freely? Neville asked about her in a letter of his own. That peevish young person did eventually learn to dance, but she ran off with a penniless curate, much to her papa's indignation.

Chapter 6

Ten years later . . .

Neville lined up his sons and daughters on opposite sides of the Abercorn ballroom. He had three of each, and a pretty picture they made in sashes and silk, the boys in breeches and the girls in long skirts. They stood with their hands clasped in front of them, looking down at the parquet floor.

"Please pay attention. We shall dance . . . a minuet."

The German music master raised his hands over the keys of the pianoforte and awaited his cue.

"Papa—must I?" Robert asked. "I would rather chase rabbits. I never catch them, but it is excellent exercise."

"So is dance," Neville said patiently.

"The minuet is old-fashioned, Papa." That was the voice of Amaryllis, who seemed to have been born to be fashionable.

"It will teach you good posture, my dear."

"No dance," said Katherine Mary. She was the smallest and only three.

"You are excused, Katherine. Run along and find your mama."

The little girl stuck out her tongue at her brothers and sisters and walked past them with her button nose in the air.

"That will do, Katherine," Neville called.

She took to her heels, laughing.

The remaining five stood where they were, but their father noted the mutinous expressions on their faces. Robert, Amaryllis, Georgina, William, Freddy—and the departed Katherine—did none of his children share his love of dance?

He looked at the music master, who still had not touched the keyboard. "That is enough for today, Mr. Herzlich."

The music master put his hands in his lap and winked at the children.

"Do not encourage them, if you please. They are rebellious enough as it is. I would not be at all surprised if they were planning a palace coup."

The children rushed him all at once. Neville was pummeled by the boys and kissed by the girls. "Have you no respect for your aged father?" he cried. "How the world has changed since I was a boy!"

His father, now an old, old man, came slowly into the grand room, leaning on his stick. "You were just as mischievous, Neville. I have not forgotten your boyhood."

Neville waved a hand and sent all the children out to play. "Go! Bring me a rabbit, Rob! No—bring me two rabbits. Then we will have an infinite supply."

"Yes, sir!" Robert was the last through the door but not the slowest, once out.

"My dear Papa—how are you feeling today? Come, let us walk together."

The old man shook his head. "I think I would rather sit with your mama in the garden and watch things grow."

"But the sun might be too warm behind its walls, Papa."

"Pooh. I refuse to sit inside and rot."

"But it is not as if you or anyone can see things growing," Neville said.

"I know that they are growing and that is enough for me."

Neville shook his head. The old man still won most of the arguments he started.

"Let us find the ladies, my boy. I enjoy their company. Your wife is always doing something interesting."

Penelope had taken up gardening of late, and there were greenhouses and flowerbeds everywhere Neville looked. He saw a large straw hat bobbing along on the other side of the garden wall and walked ahead of his father to see if it was she.

He looked over the wall. It was not. Katherine Mary held her mother's hat on a stick and moved it along the top of the wall.

"Where is your mother, my love?"

The little girl dropped the stick and the hat into a pile of leaves and pointed. Yes, that was Penelope's beautiful bottom. He would know it anywhere. The rest of her was bent over a raised flowerbed, and the dirt was flying.

"Mama!" Katherine called.

Penelope straightened.

"Daddy's here."

"Oh, hello, Neville. I thought you were teaching the children the minuet." She wiped the dirt from her face with the sleeve of her smock and came over to the wall.

"They would rather chase rabbits, my dear. What are you doing?"

"Making mudpies with Katherine." She pointed with her trowel to a neat row of patted lumps on the ground nearby and gave him an enchanting smile.

Amazing. He loved her more than ever. After ten years of marriage. Six children. The joys and sorrows of gaining and losing dear friends and relations. Life in all its glory.

"Let me wash up. I will waltz with you, Neville. It will be nice to have the ballroom to ourselves for a change."

"I would like that very much. But I have found a sure way to keep the children out of it."

"And what is that?" Penelope inquired.

"Dress them up, play music, and try to teach them something."

The old earl reached the garden wall at last. "Good morning, Penelope. I seem to have mislaid my countess and I am very fond of her. Have you seen her?"

Penelope pointed again with her trowel. "She is reading in the arboretum."

"Of course. Mama's favorite spot," Neville said.

"And mine," his father said. He set off, refusing assistance and relying on his stick. "We shall sit together. Side by side."

Neville watched the old man make his slow way across the grass and turned back to smile at Penelope.

"Side by side. I like the sound of that," she said.

"So do I." He saw that little Katherine was ab sorbed in making mudpies again and he leaned over the garden wall to kiss his own dear wife.

Very thoroughly.

More Regency Romance
From Zebra

More Historical Romance From
Jo Ann Ferguson